The Reluctant Sun

The Reluctant

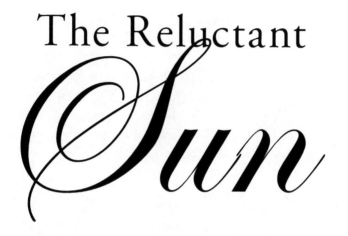

Sun

P. Emkay

PARTRIDGE

To order additional copies of this book, contact
Partridge India
000 800 10062 62
orders.india@partridgepublishing.com

www.partridgepublishing.com/india

The author is a Medical doctor, Anesthesiologist and Pain Therapist, authored many books and short stories. Worked in India, Trinidad and Tobago, England, Ireland, Denmark, Sweden and Norway as Anesthesiologist and Pain therapist.

Ever since I returned to India, I joined an interesting group of walkers on the beach. Every day morning we gather on the beachfront of Visakhapatnam's RK Beach and spend two hours in walking and an hour on chatting away all sorts of topics.

I read the news of a mysterious murder of a young woman in Boston that involved people of Indian origin and that too of Telugu descent. The victim was the daughter of a very high official who worked in our city some years back.

He immediately switched over to another topic, the smog-hidden sun and the chill in the air.

"It is chilly this morning" Murthy commented while briskly rubbing his hands. "Yeah it is cold" I walked with my hands in my pockets.

"For the last four or five days the weather is like the unpredictable English weather." He commented casually.

"Yes it is dull, dreary, lifeless and lazy ambience prevailing all over. In fact, vagaries of English weather, I must admit, drove me out of that country."

"It is like the weather of England" I made a casual comment not expecting any attention.

"Oh. Really" - Murthy sounded sarcastic; I could not but perceive some skepticism on his voice.

"I can vouch that, because I lived in England for a few years," I argued as my other friends started watching us. "During my stay in England, sunshine is a rare blessing of the heavens," I restated my opinion.

"Why then you stayed there for so long" he piercingly looked at me. I guess my words provoked Murthy, who regards England very high.

"For money; Nothing else" I blurted as if I am snubbing Murthy.

"What do you mean? He looked at me as though I am lying.

"I went to England for better emoluments. That is what I said" I was curt and dry. Afterwards I mellowed down sensing his displeasure. Murthy looked peeved.

"No I am not exaggerating Murthy. Honestly, I had gone there to make extra bucks." Murthy appeared unconvinced.

"Despite what you say I must admit my stay in England for three months is a delightful experience. I must say I had a wonderful time. I loved the weather, the people and their culture," Murthy began his eulogy of England. Although I realized that he would not change his mind I did not give up.

"I lived there for more than seven long years. Infested by labor strikes, racial disharmony UK became a reluctant host to South Asians, although they needed us. Thatcher's 'Culture swamp' comment and Enoch Powel's 'Rivers of Blood' speech frightened me and many.

I substantiated my argument with well known facts. Murthy appeared indifferent to hear my comments but I continued. "As you rightly said, England is good for visitors but not for settlers. But the fact is, the English weather is not that comfortable." "The world over knows that" I added.

However, Murthy did not pay any attention to my words. As England is the only foreign country he ever visited, he is ultra proud about his three-month tenure at government's expense. I understood that he would not like to hear my criticism as he really fancied his three-month experience of 'glorious' England. Therefore, I hesitated to continue on the theme of sunshine. Others in my group wanted to enjoy my denigration of Murthy but I stopped abruptly.

Incidentally, Murthy is an occasional walker member of our group. He is retired from active service, and was a former colleague of Ramlu; former District Collector of Vizag.

"It didn't ring a bell in me yesterday when you were talking about Ramlu. I remember his wife Rani, that vivacious and voluptuous looking woman" Murthy chuckled. In the din of noise, I could hardly hear him.

A little while later, another member, Sarma joined us. He looked into the sky and said, "After all, planets around the earth are influencing many aspects of our living including our personality and behavior." "Human behavior is similar to the hide and seeks game of the Sun" he was casual but his comment attracted our attention.

He sounded irrelevant at first but later realized that his sharp and specific words were aimed at the news report I was talking about.

"Look at Ramlu's life, a distinguished officer and an upright man. How could one expect that his daughter gets murdered in a foreign country?"

"You know Ramlu then? "In fact I was to ask if some one knew about him."

"Yes. He was that unfortunate man, a former District Collector of Vizag." "I knew him as a trainee officer and later as District Collector of Vizag and much later as Chief Secretary of our government's finance ministry."

In fact, Ramlu married a beautiful woman but not a wife. His father-in-law was a District Court Judge during the British times. He lost his wife after the birth of his daughter Rani and she hardly knew him. And now look at the fate of Ramlu's darling daughter, she faced violent death."

"I met Ramlu three times - once to convey my greeting soon after his marriage and three years later I met him in Vizag on some official matter but the third meeting was about my son's passport issue. When I told him about the premature death of my wife he felt very sad but revealed the truth about his wife Rani's social misbehavior. He made a painful comment. I wish she is dead and gone." I noticed his agony and pitiful state. He told me in sad tone "I am a lonely man; never knew what marital bliss is."

"Therefore I staunchly believe planets around the earth are influencing many aspects of our living including our personality and behavior." "Human behavior is similar to the hide and seeks game of the Sun." he concluded emphasizing his words.

Almost all of us endorsed his comment except Vasu who looked cynical. Noticing Vasu's dissenting looks, Sarma raised his voice and said "Yes. In fact, the ancient Indian astrologers were the first ones making those observations. Since ages our astrologers are known to be making *Panchangam,* (Hindu calendar), preparing *Jataka chakra* (astrological birth charts) and predict the future as per planetary position." He reflected his authority on the matters concerning astrology, which provoked Vasu's resentment.

"You don't need to know astrology that lack of sunshine makes people dull-headed," he displayed clear aversion.

Let me introduce Vasu, a senior Lawyer, enjoys arguing; he was engaged as an Advocate championing the divorce petition of Rani. Vasu claimed her father Danny, "He urged me secretly not to insist on divorce. Rani's father, Danny was a retired Vizag district court judge. I sensed that Rani's family was weird."

"Don't tell me it is all because of planets. They are mentally unstable." He argued with Sarma.

He continued arguing against Sarma. "That is all humbug Sir. Do you seriously believe that? Vasu abruptly stopped Sarma. But, Sarma's stubborn looks muted Vasu.

"Yes I do. In fact, I consider our planets decide our fate. Therefore I celebrate my birthdays as per *tidhi and nakshatram*, (position of the celestial star and planets at the time of birth) unlike others who celebrate on their birthdays on Western calendar day of birth."

Unrelenting Vasu responded with more sarcasm. "Oh really," shrugged his shoulders with an expression of contempt and surprise. He argued, "Index of suspicion must be high for a legal professional, otherwise, he becomes ineffective. It is my professional acumen and natural reaction in relation to litigation," he paused and said, "I guess I am habituated to it," he explained his stand.

"I for one do not give any credence to what Sarma says."

In the context of another discussion, Vasu expressed his disappointment with astrologers. Considering himself as agnostic, he commented – "*Evidence based* religion is what I prefer.

In response to what Vasu said, "Look at some events that spring from nowhere," Sarma claimed, "Let us take the example of Ramlu and his daughter. Do they deserve such hardships? They are rich; they are beautiful and powerful too. But look at their fate"

"If Sarmaji is right why couldn't he warn Ramlu." "He would have had better planning, to ward himself off the bad effects, protect against dangers etc."

"Despite lack of evidence, our astrologers continues to make tall claims, about their predictions mentioned in *panchangam* (Hindu calendar)." "In my opinion, it is a gross waste of time and effort. Man must make his own destiny, should not attribute any mysterious force. Life on Earth is nothing but enduring fight for survival; life is not like peeling a banana skin and eats neatly." Murthy sermonized. But, Sarma remained silent, appeared indifferent to the comments made by Vasu and Murthy; many in our group appeared uneasy and tried to disengage themselves from the discussion. Most of us kept quite.

Despite all the differences, our daily dose of deliberations sweet or sour, we keep our ritualistic morning walk. We continue to gather in the early hours of the morning and keep walking and talking until breakfast time.

Twenty-five years back the beach road was a narrow single lane road. It got improved during Ramlu's tenure. He In fact who ordered the development of our walking path. It is a stretch of three kilometers each way, a walk from Indian Navy's Coastal Battery to Park Hotel.

"I can now reveal how I got to know. I found Rani, wife of Ramlu meddling in the affairs of government. She would behave aggressively to get away with her decision." "In fact, the context was to get the works contract granted to my favorite friend. She asked me to meet her in the famous Waltair Club's Ball Room. Since she was a passionate lover of all good things in life, I could easily wine and dine her. I used different means to make her commit that she could get the approval of the tender offer of my Contractor friend," Murthy glorified himself in his accomplishment. "Since Ramlu refused, she manipulated the Deputy collector to sign the approval." Murthy cheekily smiled.

Sarma advised us "To ward off any evil you must offer prayers to Sidha Purushas (humans possessing Divine powers) like Annamayya" he advised us many times that was why. And we take a pause for a few minutes near the statue of Annamayya to offer our salutation to the Great Saint Singer of 14th century.

"Annamayya's every breath is a song in praise of Lord Venkateswara," Sarma commented. "It is difficult to estimate the greatness of Annamayya."

In fact, he is a landmark in Telugu literature. He wrote more than 30000 songs in praise of the Lord of Seven Hills, Tirupathi. All his songs convey profound philosophy and yearning for *mukti* (salvation).

When I was working with Ramlu I begged him to join me in the worship of gods. Later I appealed him to promote Annamayya's songs when he was working as the Secretary of the Hindu Endowment Department. He never believed in God and he ignored my appeal all along.

"If he had followed my advice he may have easily overcome his grief. I really feel sorry for him." Sarma always differed with his atheistic views.

Among many topics of our discussion, the most frequent topic is about political news of the day. One day a passerby commented, "Of what use it is shouting or yelling at those unreliable public enemies? You know these politicians; they are self-seeking lot, busy making money and hovering around power-centers for their political future."

"But democracy demands our participation," Rao lectured us. "But for what use except losing our breath" I joined in the argument with Rao.

"Get ready sir - soon they will descend on us with all sorts of sops and unrealistic promises; they may be deaf and dumb until now but from now on, their shrill voices make us dumb and deaf - we will become victims of the din and dust of their canvassing and boring speeches," he shot back.

Among our members Rao, the former Head of Political affairs wing of All India Radio was a former colleague of

Ramlu. He was vaguely aware of the family affairs of Ramlu but did not expect them to become so serious.

"An officer like Ramlu is rare, he never succumbed to politician's pressure," he told us.

"He was one who never allowed politicians playing dirty games; he was indeed a nightmare to his corrupt colleagues. Not just that; he was a tower of strength for people like us. He greatly inspired us by precept and practice." "I assume his enemies may have conspired to avenge their anger in this dastardly way. He was a champion of honesty, simplicity and efficiency." "What we need is awareness of our rights and duties to our nation." Every one in our area knows Rao as a vociferous critic and staunch supporter of people's rights. He is known for his strong views.

"What Manmohan Singh did to us is awful: kept us steeped in the political calumny of our country." Rao triggered us to think.

However, haughty Murthy disagreed with almost all of us and Rao in particular. Nonetheless, our friends and some of our acquaintances also concurred with Rao.

The other day ever jubilant Rao greeted us saying, "Manmohan Singh's government will be facing serious test in the ensuing elections" Rao sounded emphatic and appeared floating in high spirits.

"But public memory is short Raoji" Sarma sounded cynical.

"I will be the happiest man," Sarma and me cheered him lustily.

"Any way, I agree with you, Parliament elections in 2014 will be a life and death crisis for Congress" Vasu voiced his opinion.

Murthy got irritated "I totally disagree with you, your ideas are far-fetched," he objected vehemently.

"Murthy loves everything Western (meaning Sonia Gandhi)" Vasu remarked cryptically; Rao did not allow Murthy to continue any further. "The facts are glaring at us Mr Murthy sir. You can't ignore the facts" Rao strongly differed with him.

General elections are fast approaching; press reports indicate moneybags are changing hands. The money stacked in the strong vaults is coming out.

Sarma calmly heard our conversation and added his frustration "That is why they say 'we get what we deserve'. We are the ones to blame. We are encouraging these leaders to make us fools. Money bags have already decided the results."

"While we were walking - introspecting seriously with our heads bent, suddenly emerged Sastry approaching us with a placard hanging on his neck. "Save the nation." says a placard in the neck of Sastry the seventy year old Congress veteran. "I am fed up of this party" he admitted before we uttered any word.

"Behen Italianoji, and her cronies have finally achieved their objective. They destroyed India" his disdain and contempt are obvious on his face.

"Advantage Italianos Sastriji" shouted Tarun, the tennis enthusiast cum player briefly stopped in front of Sastry while jogging..

"India is destroyed," an impatient Vasu shouted.

"Thanks to Baba Mowni Singh, sinister Chid, the Iron legged Rahul, foul-mouthed Diggy Raja and his cohorts."

Sastry cursed each one of them, pretended spitting on their imagined face.

"In our country, Congress and Communists brand any Indian hailing 'Nation-first' slogan as communalist, fascist, and Hindu fundamentalist."

While we were slowly walking and talking in a serious mood suddenly some strangers surrounded us. They appeared aggressive, pulled out Sastry's placard, and tore the paper placard; pushed him to a side. This sudden altercation surprised many walkers on the beach; many people gathered around us - tempers flared up between those loyalists of the ruling party and the non-party public. The public intervened and chased the strangers away; we heaved a sigh of relief. This strange and stray incident certainly shook us.

Anyhow, my main attraction to beach walking is watching many people mostly cheerful young men and women.

They appeared exhilarated walking happily, some making amorous gestures to each other. They may be holidaymaking youngsters, some may be lovers but they appear like newly weds, because I could see *mehindi* (bridal decoration with henna paste) marks on the hands and feet of young brides. And, some of them wear Mattelu (toe rings), sign of marriage, besides decoration of their hands and feet with Gorintaku (Henna).

Surely, Vizag reminds me of French Riviera the beautiful French coast. I was to tell this to my friends, but immediately realized that it might sound like bragging about my familiarity with foreign countries, which is irrelevant and perhaps provoking.

In the exhilarating ambience of morning Sun and cool breeze, I rephrased my remarks – "Vizag is a fascinating city. In fact, every city in India is a myriad mix of many cultures and languages. It is indeed an inspiring land."

However, our advocate friend Vasu has a different take. He remained silent until then. "In these days, the sun reluctantly peeps at us because of pollution and smog in the air," he countered.

"The best days of Vizag were when Ramlu was the District Collector." Vasu concluded; compliments about his uncle pleasantly surprised Murli. Nevertheless he did not reveal his connection with him.

"It is worse in other cities. Hyderabad is now becoming unlivable, you know," Murli lamented.

We later realized that Murli played such a big role in the unpublicized story of Lena's affair with Krish.

Murli continued "I do think the environment in Vizag is much better you know. Although I am from Telangana region, I chose Vizag as my permanent abode for another reason; I found truth in the claim that people in Vizag are low-profiled and docile. In fact, people of my native district Adilabad are also the same kind."

"Above all, Vizag has the vast expanse of the sea; its constant 'yearning' to cross the coast fascinated me. The gusty sound waves, gentle breeze and the constantly changing images keep you absorbed. I love the sight of morning's rising sun." Murli sounded very appreciative.

"But I noticed the reluctance of the sun to shine." I have been waiting and watching for the sun to rise; it is now more than four or five days," he pointed at the eastern horizon. "The gloomy dusky ambience is not welcome anymore … four days have gone" I talked as if I could order better weather.

"We almost forgot the gleam and glitter of sunny mornings," complained Mohan of a software technology company. "For some odd reason the Sun is unwilling to visit the earth here" frustrated Mohan looked at Srinivas, the retired meteorologist.

Srinivas stopped us, and said, "Nothing is odd about the Sun. We, the inhabitants of Earth are at fault; we polluted even the ethereal zone." He screamed through his clogged voice. He recently retired from central government's meteorology department but he enjoys talking scientifically about weather. He rarely approves our comments about weather because he knows more about it as a serious scientific issue. However he is always eager to throw light on weather changes with an obvious in-depth scientific knowledge.

"No Srinivas, Sun also is becoming lazy like the modern people, waking up late may be" chuckled Murthy.

Another talking point among our walkers group is about independent living, and avoid living with children. We resolved and not to talk about reluctant sons.

"Let us encourage ourselves to keep independent despite the fact we are all nearing our seventies." However, some of us do raise some practical questions: what if we fall sick suddenly? Vasu questioned.

"Yes we are vulnerable but there are solutions to every problem," I declared. The Western world has already gone through this problem, we could learn from their experience," I tried convincing my friends. "We harbor wrong notions about old-age homes, but, I can tell you that bias is wrong. Their Old age homes are luxurious five-star abodes with every facility you can think of unlike our makeshift, ill-made dirty old age homes."

"Let us therefore think of developing Indian variety of *vanaprasthas* (Retirement abodes)."

"Is it practical in our country?

"Nothing is impractical if we set our mind to it" I affirmed my faith. We kept discussing about our old age and health insecurities.

"I wonder why we should be living under the shelter of our children," Rao posed a question. He looked at us proudly and declared in a confident voice "Most of us already started living by ourselves. So far we are caring each other and managing very well," he pointed at us.

"We should not blame children as we are not prepared to live under the shelter of someone else; even if that someone is our own," I declared emphatically. But our friend Sarma's case is grossly different. It is a case of utter neglect and ingratitude.

Sarma did not wish to go to US even though he was alone and had none to help him except his friends.

"I do not wish to go to USA." Sarma did not hide his anger cantankerous. "Him America made a reluctant son out of a good boy. I have lost him to America" he thus voiced his resentment of America. It was not pleasant to hear such comments made by a pious man.

He was a teacher of Mathematics, although retired from service he is ever ready to offer free tuition to poor and underprivileged students. However, Sarma rarely talked about himself or his career. Nevertheless, I wanted to know more about him.

"What use is it? I am after all a schoolteacher; you guys are big big officers. I have nothing to brag," he tried to evade answering me. After great persuasion and probing, he talked a little about himself.

While narrating the story about himself he jokingly started. "I started my career with an 'award of punishment' I asked him why.

He laughed, "For rejecting mass copying in which a Minister's son was involved and since I caught him red-handed. The authority instructed me to withdraw my recommendation of debarring those boys from school. I refused to oblige. Local 'negotiators' and a senior IAS officer descended from Hyderabad on behalf of the minister. He tried to reason with me saying this is after all first year intermediate exam and that I should not spoil their career."

"I refused to budge, stood my ground and the IAS officer got furious with me. He gave me a stern warning. 'Mr Sarma, you will suffer the consequences for defying me. I can book you for being caste-biased. I observed you are anti-Dalits'. I looked at him deep into his eyes, raging with anger told him directly, "You are shameless and mean and you insult Goddess Saraswati. Calling yourself an Educator is an utter shame. Do what you want to do. I will not retract my complaint." I walked out of his office.

Pat came, the transfer order. Because of my defiance, I was transferred immediately pending further action, from my hometown Vizag to the tribal Chintapalli area. That disturbed my family a great deal but, it was god sent for me; there I met an honest young IAS officer Ramlu. He worked hand-in-hand with me and developed the high school, proved himself an upright honest dedicated and ideal Officer. He acted ruthlessly against erring teachers and disorderly students. The secret I got to know later is that Ramlu, the IAS Officer is a Tribal himself, he is from Adilabad district, I believe. He was unmarried at that time and acted without any fear or favor." Murli did not reveal his identity, as he was proud to hear such nice comments about his uncle.

"What about your family and children? I asked him quite casually.

Sarma placed his two hands on the handle of the walking stick leaned forward and glanced at me with artificial smile.

"Should I have to tell you? A streak of sadness and subdued emotion gripped him unprepared. He turned his face away from me and mumbled some words. I noticed his unease in answering.

"The School authorities have done a lot of damage to my life. My wife and me had to stay in different places. She had to stay in the city for the sake of my son's schooling. It seriously disturbed the stability of our family." "In the process I could not communicate with my son properly and be a caring father" he swallowed some words.

He tried to resist tears, "My only child is a 'lost son' to me. He migrated to US after marrying an American based Indian girl. Strangely, that girl is a niece of Rani. In fact, she is a distant cousin of my best friend Ramlu too."

It so happened that I had to seek his help to get passport for my son. We both went to his home in Hyderabad; there my son 0Subbu met their niece Santa Di and fell in love with her at first site. My son by then got admission to pursue postgraduate studies in MIT, USA.

Since Santa already migrated to USA with her parents became a Naturalized Citizen of America. Needless to say, but Santa Di and Rani lured my son with American Dream; he fell into the trap never to return. They took him away from me forever," he bewailed.

"I am not against any race or religion but that woman is very special, her behavior is worse than that of Rani. She smokes, drinks, and walks in skimpy clothes. She turned my son into her personal servant and financier of her luxurious life style; he also drinks. He religiously follows his socialite wife to every party." For the first time, I saw an old distraught, grief stricken angry Sarmaji.

"I have no contact with them. It is more than 10 years since I saw Subbu." He hit his walking stick on the ground and suddenly got up from the cement bench seat looking utterly dejected. I was listless for a moment.

"I am sorry Sarma. I raked up a healing wound."

"Oh, no, wounds heal quickly when they are aired." Sarma calmly smiled and made a profound statement, "Fate is not bound by expectation, hope or reason."

So much agony behind the smiley face of Sarma!

A few months back Sarma introduced me to another interesting man, Vyas. "I am lucky to have such a nice neighbor. He takes good care of me. He and his wife are like children to me."

"Meet Captain Vyas" Sarma introduced a retired army man; a staunch nationalist and a great patriot. He won several awards for his bravery in the Indian Army." "He lives in the same apartment block as me." Vyas folded his hands and greeted us with a gentle smile.

"Sarmaji is like a father to me." Vyas's pale complexion and facial features indicate he must be from the North of India.

Vyas speaks to us mostly in English with a spat of Telugu words ill pronounced. "Although my father is a Telugu person, he spoke only Hindi. He died as a martyr when I was hardly seven years old. My mother hails from Meerut in UP."

While my father was a soldier in Subhas Chandra Bose's Indian National Army, Rani's grandfather was a soldier in the British Army. The rumor is that they confronted each other in the Second World War in Burmese territory and were killed in the same battleground in Burma.

"My father hails from Andhra region," he proudly mentioned that he has Telugu heritage.

Vyas now is a retired army Captain by profession; claims he worked in Kargil during the war with Pakistan. As I was deeply interested in hearing the Kargil war stories, I got close to him. He related many fascinating stories about the Indian Army's Valor.

I noticed his eagerness to tell his war experiences; "I started in the army as foot soldier and front liner but survived the war. I am still alive due to grace of God and rose to Captain's rank," he proudly told me.

"Let me tell you about an episode. During the Kargil war, a few of us were to clear mines before the team of engineers begins to build tracks, bridges and bunkers. While I set on scouting, I suddenly, confronted face to face with a bearded Pathan (Afghani) fellow who appeared very weak and emaciated. I noted he could hardly lift his gun. Somehow, he managed to lift the gun, point bayonet at me and threatened to kill me if I advanced one inch further. I looked at him in his eyes and challenged him boldly.

"If you have, guts fight with me - if not surrender; I will get you protected as POW. Poor fellow depleted of ammunition and badly injured leg he instantly surrendered, dropped his gun begged me "please get me to a hospital, get my leg amputated. It is rotten."

I pulled him out of the mud-filled pit, carried him on my shoulders to the base, my boss greatly appreciated my humane gesture gave me a commendation letter."

"How could you recognize he was from enemy side? One of our friends sneakily questioned the veracity of his story.

"First of all the Afghan Mujahedeen's are mercenaries, they are paid by the fanatic Saudi Arabian oil sheiks. They do not wear any uniform; secondly, they speak Pashtu language only. Besides, there are many other technical ID methods."

Like this, the stories related by Vyas were awesome for us.

One more member of our group Appaji, also had Army experience but discharged on grounds of health. "Soon after my engineering, I joined the army as junior commissioned officer, but, shifted to civil service within two years. It happened 48 years back, but even today, I regret I made a grave mistake in my life. I do not know why my enthusiasm for army service was short, in all, less than two years." Appaji appeared rueful. "I cheated the army by pretending bad health. My uncle gave me the tips though."

"You need to have a mindset to work in regimental services," Vyas quipped.

"The biggest wrong step I ever made was to join the Civil service, in my 20 years of government service

"I must admit I fell into the well-laid trap of an intermediary and his mistress, a keep, a bitch. I regret I fleeced the state exchequer of a few crore rupees." "I know I am not innocent but I am not the monetary beneficiary of any of the transactions that took place within my authority." "I fell into the cesspool of corruption. Finally I was in the news papers for wrong reasons, ACB (Anti Corruption Bureau) got me and I faced arrest and dismissal." His face reflected signs of self-pity, remorse and regret. The deep furrows on the skin of his forehead are perhaps the scars of long-lasting guilt, doubt and penitence.

He appears to be holding several secrets boxed in his head; must be strangling his freedom, I felt.

"I have a brother who is bed ridden due to severe joint problems." "He is fed up of life. He showed me the suicide note he wrote." He told me "I begged my indifferent wife to give me some poison." Impenitently, his wife accused him of conspiracy to get her arrested. She told me, "Your brother is mad. He wants to take his revenge on me. Earlier he wrote a suicide note mentioning that I am responsible for his misfortune and death. I know his cunningness. He deserves a painful death." She gnawed her teeth in anger. Nevertheless, his daughters kept trying to keep the parents together."

Appaji continued in a complaining manner. I wanted to ask her, "Haven't you eloped with my brother and forced him to marry you. You weaned him away from us. Have you forgotten how much ill treatment you meted out to my parents?

"Since I have no guts, I never could ask," he said. "Fortunately, neither does a devilish wife harass me nor am I wheel chaired." However, she refused to allow me to visit him either. That guilt bothers me a lot."

However, the fact is Appaji lost on all counts. He says he is living on paltry sums of money he saved. He often revealed with bitterness how he ruined himself. "I am born loser. I gained nothing from life" his bitterness is visible on his face.

"My wife died young. My son disowned me. If I recount the sacrifices I made for him, I feel I am cheated more by my own son than by that bitch, that 'keep', I hooked to."

"Did I tell you this; I lost my wife when I was hardly forty years. Since then I have not contemplated remarriage: I sincerely believed in the *seven oaths* I gave to my wife. I cannot annul that promise I made to her. Therefore, I have opted not to remarry. I devoted myself to my son Vinay, loaned six lakh rupees (0.6 million) to educate him in USA. Now that he abandoned me, I had to repay the loan made for his education."

"My son too has a share in the tragedy affecting Ramlu," confessed Appaji, "While studying in New York he got into love affair with the daughter of Ramlu. Lucky for him she hooked another man, one of my son's classmates."

Another interesting man is Rani's cousin who Sunny lives in Vizag; Sunny is a pet name of Kali, the nephew of Rani's father Danny. Sunny and Appaji were good friends not only in the office but also in playing card-game Rummy. Murali knows him well.

Sunny tried arguing in support of Appaji; raised his voice and said, "In a competitive world choosing the right recipients for the government sops, is not that easy. The system gives us discretionary powers. Therefore, you extend the benefit to whomever you know. People may name it as corruption. Should we call it corruption? Recipients of our favor feel that as 'token' of their gratitude, money if you like." Silent Sunny rarely speaks his mind.

"What the hell you mean? Completely changed impatient Appaji questioned Kali. "Corruption is corruption. It bleeds the society of all its moral and material wealth. It promotes deceit, dishonesty and disobedience. Condoning corruption is an immoral, illegitimate act. Corruption breeds corruption. Corruption may fill the pockets of a few *Babus* (officers) but empties the dinner plates of thousands of poor people. More than anything it debilitates the society," Appaji reacted angrily as he very much repented his past.

'Sunny can fix it' was the adage in his office. 'Sunny can manage anybody and any problem' were the remarks you hear about him from his colleagues. Besides, he is a Houdini in escaping from any difficulty."

Sadly, Rani's father Danny fell for his nephew's maneuvers and got discredited at the end of his distinguished career. Therefore my uncle Ramlu never allowed him to come near him. Nevertheless, Sunny tried every trick in the trade to get my uncle bribed. He tried another route, through aunty Rani. I must say he chose the wrong route."

"Corruption is his compulsive desire. There is no need for him to do wrong things to make more money. He is financially rich, has neither burdens nor responsibilities, except managing his medical problem, the punishing attacks of severe Asthma."

"His insatiable greed and thirst for money is legendary, I am always scared of him" uncle Ramlu warned me "Sunny gets a vicarious pleasure if he can put you into wrong doing without your knowing." I assured myself, fortunately, I have no use of his special skills. I meet him in a group and leave him there; I strictly followed the advice of my uncle.

Murli always introduced himself as nephew of Ramlu, the great District Collector of Vizag who worked with our Sarma and many other Vizagites. He served in this district for three years in various capacities and earned good name.

"My uncle frequently talked about Vizag. His fond memories of this town influenced me a lot," Murli reminisced.

Upon my request, Murli told us his reason for settling in Vizag. He began his story with a sad beginning.

"I followed my wife Smitha's advice, purchased a small seaside apartment near my in-laws house. Poor Smitha did not live long to enjoy her own house. A few years back she died of cancer. The sweet memories of her haunt me every time I sit on the beach sands alone. For a long time after her

The Reluctant Sun

death, I was searching for a glimpse of her image. In fact, that was my incentive to go to the beach. To my misfortune, we did not have any children. Nor do I have any of my near relation here in Vizag." "Since Smitha's parents were migrants from the North, they also do not have any relatives either. Therefore, I look upon walker friends as my family. I enjoy taking rounds regularly and visit them at their homes quite often." We appreciated Murli's sentiments.

What about Ramlu, the past District Collector? We asked Murli. "It is a complex mix of people, places and events. I will tell you next time we meet" Murli briefly replied.

Although the sun's reluctance bothered us all waiting for Murli's story kept us going till the next morning.

Murli continued, "Interestingly uncle Ramlu and this city are also connected through many friends. Vinay's father Appaji is one of them. In fact, uncle Ramlu tried to restrain Appaji from wrongdoing. Now that you all know Appaji let me talk about his son, Vinay first. I and Vinay were classmates in Ahmedabad's Indian Institute of Management. We were good friends because we both are from Andhra Pradesh, speaking the same language.

Strangely, Vinay never revealed that he is from Vizag. It was somewhat unusual about Vinay; he never revealed his father's

27

name or his home address. Most of us in our student-days, were exchanging our addresses, extend invitations etc. In IIM Ahmadabad students from our state are by far very few.

We also noticed that Vinay preferred to stay back in the hostel than go home during college's holidays. Whenever we asked Vinay why he would not go to his native place for holidays, he would evade answering.

I do not know about the others but I was curious to know the reasons. However, one day Vinay voluntarily confided in me "I am not proud of my father. I lost my mother when I was three years old. Our relations claim that my mom's death was unnatural; someone told me she committed suicide. Our family knew my father as wayward, corrupt and a sex-maniac.

His office colleagues told me he could easily trap a woman and make her his sex slave. Every time I go home, I would have to greet a new lady-friend of his.

Looking at this *tamasha*, I begged him to marry again." His standard reply was, 'which bride will marry a forty five year-old man? He used to give some plausible explanations to continue his Casanova escapades," Vinay's tired, sad face conveyed his deep anguish.

Vinay told me later that his dad suddenly lost the 'favor of lady-luck'. "He fell into the trap of corruption and adultery." He told us that a young woman and her broker 'husband' (cum politician) started blackmailing him, made him sign some false papers for a consideration. ACB, Anti Corruption Bureau caught him red-handed and jailed him.

"That bitch living with him relieved all his cash and other valuables, while he was in jail and left him empty handed." "He thus lost everything, spent a year in jail, officially disgraced and socially rejected; all our family members abandoned us, especially family people keep him at a distance for fear of getting cheated."

"Mom passed away when I was hardly 3 years. I do not know how she looks like. I only heard from our friends that she was always soft-spoken and mild mannered. Since I have a disgraced father and deceased mother I have none at home in Vizag."

Vinay was one among five more in our friends group. Of all Krish is the most handsome, outspoken and friendly person. We are all Telugu speaking students living in hostels.

Our group mate Krishnamachary, Krish for short is the son of a Scientific Advisor serving some central government organization. He had his primary and secondary schooling in Rishi Valley School, Madanapalli. One must attribute all the finesse of his personality to his schooling in Rishi Valley. We greatly admired him.

After our IIM days were over, we got placements in different organizations, lost touch with each other. Luckily, Vinay and Krish were in New York at the same time.. Krish came to study in NY as a service candidate from Accenture. Vinay also was studying in NY.

An year before, Ramlu's daughter Lena began her studies in New York. In fact, Vinay was her classmate in NY and I too I came to NY to work for Tata Consultancy Services.

Unexpectedly, uncle Ramlu was visiting his daughter in NY, precisely at the same time; which, turned out to be a significant event.

It was a dramatic coincidence. My uncle saw Krish and Lena walking together returning from the tennis grounds. He saw Krish leaving her to reach his residence. Uncle and I saw them from a distance. He curiously asked me if I saw them.

"Yes, I saw them today also. He is Lena's tennis partner Krish." I was casual in my reply.

"Would you believe you know him too? I raked his memory "You remember Parvathi and Maheshwar your neighbors in Hyderabad - it is of course more than 20 years back." After considerable effort, Ramlu recollected Krish's parents were his neighbors in Hyderabad.

"They are an orthodox Brahmin couple, I remember" he looked into the sky, tapped his head and said, "I know them very closely because of an embarrassing incident." "I very well remember the occasion. As we were visiting them for the first time in their house, Rani and I were asked to remove shoes before entering their house. Rani considered that offensive." He paused for amoment and continued.

"What a fuss Rani made over that. She claimed that she was deeply hurt because they asked her to remove the shoes. I thought they were justified in observing some hygienic rules. After all it is their house. But Rani was extremely rude to them ever since." She always referred them as "Manner less idiots." She continued cursing them even now. But I apologized on behalf of both of us. When I told her that, she got furious and hurled unspeakable abuses.

"Past is past; I am glad to see Krish grew into a fine boy" Ramlu sincerely appreciated Krish's personality.

An hour before leaving New York uncle enquired if Krish was married. I told him "As far as I know he is still a bachelor." That information electrified Ramlu.

"Isn't he a good looking boy. Isn't he? He seemed excited, looked at his nephew for a positive answer. "He appears pretty strong and stylish, I like him very much Murli. I wish he could be my son-in-law." He appeared overwhelmed.

After a little pause he looked at me sternly, "Do me a favor, encourage Lena to get closer, have a date with him" I thought of ridiculing uncle's imagination.

"Krish is a Brahmin boy Uncle," I cautioned him.

"What sort of rubbish is this Murli! We are living in modern times" Ramlu chided me for mentioning that as a big constraint. "It is a pity I am leaving NY in a few minutes or else I could have arranged a great party to bring them together, myself."

"He deserves Lena's hand," claimed the proud father. I smiled at his ignorance of the current world.

But certainly ignited me to think positively. "Why not, they both are good-looking, look like they are made for each other. After all, she is my cousin sister too" I justified my interest in bringing them closer as suggested by my uncle.

At once, I got into action. I began working on the task I was given.

That was when I got involved in a fairy-tale neither fair nor fairy. I became an unwitting partner in the entire tragic episode. Anyhow, I started my plan of action. My first target was my friend Krish.

"You know something Krish; Lena, your tennis partner was a neighbor of yours in Hyderabad." "Can you remember this girl Krish - she is Ramlu's daughter - your neighbor in Hyderabad."

"The then director of Endowments department Ramlu's daughter?" he raised his eyebrows in utter dismay.

I was glad that the name Ramlu rang a bell in Krish. "The big burly man with a big mustache," Krish exclaimed with obvious excitement. "Yes I remember him; this girl Lena is his daughter; Krish's pleasant surprise was clearly visible.

"What a world. It is so small yaar" he appeared delighted. "Until now I knew nothing about her, except the fact that she is from our region in India." "My parents left Hyderabad when I was hardly nine years old. Nevertheless, I have faint memory of our neighbors, one remarkable lady and a big burly man, Krish sounded nostalgic.

"I could have introduced you to Ramlu, who came to visit his daughter Lena. He just left to the airport, to catch his flight back to Hyderabad."

Sensing Krish's apparent interest to know more I dared to suggest, "Shall we surprise Lena?

"Sure, let's go" he appeared anxious. I rang Lena at once and asked her if she could come down to the tennis court and meet me there, their usual joint."

"Should I come right away? Lena sounded calm and in good moods. Fortunately she did not put any counter question. While we were waiting, I observed Krish's eagerness to meet Lena.

"It is indeed a pleasant surprise to know that Lena is your cousin." Krish's readiness to meet Lena augured well. But is she ready for him -that question was hacking my mind.

When Lena arrived, Krish looked at Lena with excitement. His wandering eyes embarrassed her, "I never could imagine you are that little girl." Krish's face glowed with excitement.

"Do you know who I am" he questioned her with wonder.

"What did you say? She exclaimed, "Why do you question me like that? She countered him with a question mark on her face.

"Remember your childhood days in Hyderabad?

"What about? She looked at us with surprise and curiosity.

"Remember any of your neighbors in Hyderabad?

"Mostly I grew up in Horsely Hill Residential School. I vaguely remember my childhood days in Hyderabad" she looked at me "You know I left Hyderabad when I was hardly five or six years."

"Yes I know, but let me give you a few clues," I said with a naughty smile, "Remember a Brahmin family with a boy of my age and a tall lady, she was feeding us Idli, Sambar (south Indian dishes)" I coaxed her to think.

"Yes, I remember a tall lady offering us some special food. I remember her kindly smile. I remember her diamond nose-pin." Krish interrupted her "That lady is my mom" Krish's beaming smile said it all.

She rose from her chair. With her hands on her lips, "I can't believe this" yelled Lena with excitement.

"What a small world we live in" she hugged Krish. "Murli and I used to share some goodies we were getting from your mom. If I remember right, she is tall and wheat complexioned handsome lady. She looked very beautiful

34

and dignified." She paused a little while and said, "My mom used to chase Murli away from me but I was allowed to play with a boy; are you that boy? She wondered. Krish nodded his head briskly.

"Really," Lena yelled with awesome surprise. "You were a lanky, tall boy." She laughed loudly. "What I can't forget is the taste of her Idli and Sambar. I used to enjoy sharing that food with him" she pointed a finger at me.

"I am that boy you are allowed to play with," Krish smiled naughtily. "And the guy that got chased away by your mom is Murli. Although my dad worked there for five years, we left Hyderabad abruptly after some altercation. I was eight or nine years then." Krish made Lena recall her childhood. She profusely thanked Murli for that get-together.

"It is already late guys, I have to work tomorrow," I brought them to time sense. Lena and Krish rose from their seats.

"Sorry Murli," Krish was apologetic. Lena hugged me and bid good night to us.

"Sweet dreams Lena" Krish naughtily smiled at her while departing.

"You too," Lena waved a kiss and left.

Lena did not waste any time, rang her mother about Krish.

"I am in love mom," she was garrulous

Rani cried 'foul' the moment she heard the names of Krish's parents.

"Lena", she shouted over the phone "Brahmins are racists, I hate them, they are manner less people. Don't go near them," she vehemently objected Lena getting closer to Krish. Lena got angry with her mother and slammed the phone down.

After reaching home Ramlu heard from Lena about her dream boy. Dad I want to get married to Krish. I love him." She chatted away for more than half an hour. At the end, she added "Mom is deadly against Krish," she complained.

Ramlu shouted, "When did she behave like a mother to you? For god's sake, why did you ask her my dear Lena? He reduced his angry tone and sounded begging.

He put the phone down and went straight to her portion of the house.

"Don't you ever dare come near Lena. Don't destroy her life you stupid woman" he cursed Rani with many harsh words. She was equally rude though. Nevertheless, undeterred Rani continued her tirade against her husband.

In her classical phrases, "Your dad might ruin your life," she shouted at Lena.

"He is begging the beggar community (Brahmins). We are Raj Gondhs; we are not supposed to beg, we are meant to give orders." Rani would not allow her daughter to continue her friendship with Krish..

'I love Krish. And I don't care if you like him or not" Lena declared her intention. Since I knew her from her childhood, I predicted that.

Krish phoned his parents and conveyed his desire to marry Lena; parents Mahesh and Parvathi were shocked to hear the news.

"How on earth did you meet this girl? Mahesh fired at his son. Parvathi cautioned her husband, "Please do not to argue, handle him carefully," Mahesh could not control his anger shouted at Parvathi.

"You do not understand Mahesh - Our son is being trapped" "They must be blackmailing him" Parvathi got agitated. "I understand that she is like her mother. A kind of socialite," bewailed Parvathi.

At that juncture, I did not hesitate to jump into the fray.

"They love each other aunty," I pleaded. "No one to be blamed" I tried to counter her accusation.

Unlike Rani's bad mouthing of Parvathi and Maheshwar, Ramlu tried to please them. He pleaded with them to ignore Rani's misbehavior.

"Please accept my daughter into your family" Ramlu nearly begged Maheswar. Much before Ramlu's confrontation with Krish's parents I told uncle: "Krish is already in the hands of Lena, his parents will have to concede" I assured.

We tried convincing Krish's parents. "We are tribal people, no doubt, and, we are different from plains people. We Gondhs also do not want to mix with non-Gondhs. But here we are - Krish loves Lena; isn't that the bottom-line. We have to make concessions, sir," we appealed.

"In any case, we are equally well-educated and well placed. There is nothing more to choose" I emphasized the last words Krish's parents appeared apprehensive.

"But Rani is no easy person. She might even kill her daughter if she disagrees with her; she is that cruel. I know this from my personal experience," Parvathi expressed her fear.

Ramlu revealed to me his feelings about his estranged wife without any reservation. He even told his daughter "Your mum has a loud mouth. Don't listen to her."

"She is such a troublesome person; she is a self opinioned brute." He called her a tormenter and continued his accusation "She misused my office claiming her position as Collector's wife. She exercised more authority on my office subordinates than me." "At times I wondered if I or she is the boss for my staff. She embarrassed me with her bossy behavior while I was working in the government as District Collector."

"As a matter of fact my official Daffedar (peon) was actually leaving the office to attend on Memsahib's commands", "They were meekly submitting themselves both to my scolding and to the undue commands of Memsahib'.

Uncle warned her many times, but she would not listen. I heard him yelling at his staff "You guys are not our personal servants, you are meant for office work," but they know Ranimem would have her way. She would negate my uncle. Ramlu lamented these nasty instances many times before.

Incidentally I had on one occasion, heard Rani claiming, "He may be the Collector but I am his boss, you understand." She was overtly claiming her authority.

"I know how to make staff obey. I am the daughter of a District Court Judge," Rani openly snubbed Ramlu. "But that was British times, not viable anymore," I heard my uncle admonishing her.

The idea of marriage of Krish with non-Brahmin Lena did not sink into the minds of Krish's parents they demanded, that the marriage must be performed as per Vedic rights Maheswar insisted imagining he is still in control of his son.

"What if, if they don't believe in it? Krish nervously asked his parents. "They have to agree. In the Manu Dharma Sastra (Hindu code of conduct) the girl acquires the man's caste; hence it is imperative they follow the traditions stipulated for all Hindus."

"My foot, if I love you – do I have to love your dog? Lena explicitly spelt her opinion. "Manu Dharma is the worst practice. Manu created untouchables; created slavery and destroyed the social harmony between different people of Hindu faith. I hate the very mentioning of that name."

Parvathi and Maheswar were dumb struck. "Such a disregard? Priest Sastry felt a slap on his face.

"Why insisting on such archaic practices? Krish sounded unconvinced of Vedic rituals' importance.

"What did you say? Maheswar looked at his son grouchily. "Have you forgotten the promise you made in your upanayanam (religious initiation ritual)?

"What upanayanam dad. I was just five years old and never ever practiced the *Sandhyavandanam* (daily worship of *Surya* The Sun God) and *Gayatrimata* (mother goddess) after the ceremony. I remember only the *Gayatri mantra*. However I never saw you practicing *Sandhyavandanam* either" that statement from the mouth of his son provoked fit of anger of his father.

"Mind your tongue" Krish's father frowned. "You know very little of me" Maheswar looked deeply offended. "How much do you know of me mister? Don't ever judge others by your standards" he got up from his chair pushed it back rashly and tried to leave. Parvati restrained him. She looked at her son gently and said "We do not favor exhibitionism Krish – you may not know this; he conducts his *sandhya* worship in the privacy of the bathroom." "He is an ardent worshipper of *Gayatrimata.*" Krish bent his head looking at the stern face of his mother.

"Forgive me if I am wrong" he looked at his father.

"Since he renounced his Brahminism nothing binds him. He can do what he likes" Maheswar addressed Parvathi in a harsh tone.

"Marriage is my choice; I expected you to appreciate my choice. I do not give any importance to caste, creed or religion; and that is I. You are the one sent me to Rishi Valley School. I learnt there most of my religious morals" he added authenticity to his beliefs.

He declared very courageously "I am neither a Hindu nor Moslem nor a Christian; I am an agnostic person. I don't like to be dogmatic."

"Thank you for telling us this. Good luck with your ideas. Nevertheless, it is my duty to appeal to you – stick to your *Dharma*, do not be cruel to animals. Just because you are marrying a non-vegetarian, you don't need to convert yourself. Do not relinquish nobility and kindness toward our fellow creatures. They too have a right to live" Maheswar chastised him with added sarcasm. "We wish you very best of everything you wish for." "Our heartiest blessings to you" thus saying they both got up from their seats.

"Won't you attend my marriage? Krish looked at them with anticipation of a positive reply.

"As per our norms marriage knits families. In your case bride is from broken marriage and she has very little respect towards us. Hence, we are not sure if we have any role to play. I guess it is all yours" Krish tried to touch their feet and seek blessings; they withdrew and warned him not to bend. "Take care of your back" Maheswar quipped. Sadness wrought on his face, Parvati tried to stop sobbing, covered her mouth with the saree and left Krish's place.

I being the facilitator of the marriage of Krish with Lena can now recount the events of the story.

I recollect verbatim the naïve discussion Krish's parents had prior to marriage. Parvati and Mahesh began tutoring their son Krish about the importance of marriage: "The aim is development of new ties between hitherto unknown families. Marriage between two individuals is to knit families together. It is not just between a man and wife. In selecting our bride or bridegroom, the expected minimum requirements are sound family background and *sampradayabadhata* (observing traditions); they are our essential, basic, requirements. Rest of everything can be ignored. Although they are Hindus, their traditions are not the same as ours." I know Krish never cared to listen.

But I know they persisted in discouraging Krish, "Moreover, Lena, hails from a family of psychologically unsound people and of uneasy relationships. It appears they are neither modern nor traditional. Her socialite mother is adamant and considers Brahmins as racists and authoritative. It may sound unfair but we understand they are not averse to wife swapping and establishing second set-ups." "As per our traditions marriage is sacred; it is once a lifetime affair" Parvati enunciated the sentimental value and firm commitment to marriage.

"We heard that Lena has had several boyfriends before you entered her life. You yourself said she is not a virgin. We also heard she aborted pregnancies many times before. Forgive us if that was wrong information." Nevertheless Krish appeared unrelenting.

"I do not mind that mom. As you said marriage is spiritual not just physical. I am attracted to her heart and spirit" Krish tried to philosophize. "We have a lot in common. I love her; I don't care if she flirted with others. She is simple, straight forward and honest person. She did not conceal any of her previous relationships. I know she was deceived by some of her so-called friends."

Taken aback Maheswar got dismayed. He could not believe what he heard. "Is he of my blood? He floundered for words, looked at his wife with a blank face. Parvati grasped his hands and tried to comfort him.

"He is under the spell. He won't listen to us" Maheswar told his wife. Thus all their attempts to convince Krish failed.

"As per our traditions marriage is sacred; it is once a lifetime affair" his mother tried to persuade Krish to rethink. Parvati enunciated the sentimental value and firm commitment to marriage.

Krish was aware of the mental agony of his parents. He acknowledged later that his parents could not digest what he uttered.

Let me now narrate my role as faclitator between Lena and Krish.

On behalf of Ramlu I acted with great caution; I did not reveal that Krish is all too happy to know about his proposal. Knowing her arrogance and rashness, I cautiously approached her and wished to test the waters before proceeding any further. I tried to give her an impression that Krish may not agree. I raised a doubt and kept her guessing.

"Am I in love with Krish" Lena mused in herself. Since Murli added new dimension she became nervous. Until now, she was dictating terms to the seekers of her love, but now, she dreaded to think that Krish might reject her.

I was responsible for that element of anxiety; I had to do that.

"I will try to convince Krish" I hyped her anxiety by acting as if Krish is tough and unyielding. "You know he is Vice President of an international company before coming to NY. He is not that easy to fall for superficial beauty and charm" I tried to prick her ego bobble. Lena looked quite gloomy.

"He saw me kissing Robert, my classmate" she mused in herself. I noticed the softening mindset of Lena.

"At least, let me meet him in privacy – for example a hotel room in Waldorfs" she mumbled.

I noted Lena's longing to meet Krish in private. I understood her anxiety but decided not to give her any chance of manipulation. I met Krish in his hostel room.

"She is longing to meet you in privacy, I wish to book a room for you both to sit calmly to discuss…" Krish interrupted me saying "Not necessary." He added, "We will take a stroll in the Madison Square Garden."

"I am not going to bite you" she cajoled Krish.

"That is not the point Lena, we are mature enough to screen out each other." "It is time we exchange our ideas with each other, need to know more at personal level." Nevertheless, he firmly refused her idea of 'privacy' in a hotel room.

She had to agree to allow Krish to guide the course of action. It was a hot summer day in New York. The city was experiencing record high temperature of hundred plus that day. Many Americans were wearing goggles to shield from the bright light; most of them were half-naked for sunbathing. Lena dressed herself in tight jeans and a snug-fit T-shirt squeezing her popping bosom. She appeared stunningly beautiful and desirable.

"Let us sit in the shade of that birch tree," Krish suggested seeing Lena struggling to avoid exposure to sun. Blowing winds kept her dark shiny long hair flying in all directions. They sat close to each other.

After a few minutes, Krish broke the silence. "I would like to know what you think of me" he looked at her with wide opened staring eyes.

Unhesitatingly, Lena pronounced, "I like you very much Krish but I wonder if you really like me." Lena looked at him apprehensively. She appeared tense but excited. He sat cross-legged on the green lawn almost in squatting position. Lena sat on the lawn, stretching her long and slender legs.. She looked at him expectantly. He did not answer immediately. She removed her dark glasses cleaned them and placed them in her handbag. Before she raised her head to look at him, Krish talked provokingly.

"I guess you may be dating someone." That was Krish's first intimate comment on her. "I had seen you with Vinay…." Lena's face blushed "You are right Krish, I dated with many. I even had sex with your friend Vinay. But I did not like him. In fact, I liked none of them; I tried an Afro-American also" she blinked fast and sharply looked at Krish.

"Let me know if you feel awkward about it. I do not mind if you reject me on that ground." She looked calm but confident.

Anyhow, this was no news to Krish. "In these days it is very common; more than 70% of college boys and girls have had sex experience before marriage," he read in the national newspapers in India. Hence, Krish accepted that as non-significant news. In fact, he already got the hint from Vinay. He prepared himself to accept her sexual promiscuity.

"I don't mind that Lena; in fact I love your honesty, self-confidence, calmness and composure" he praised and paused for her reaction. She responded with a gentle smile said, "I got that from my dad. He is known for his honesty and uprightness."

Lena noticed Krish is trying to please her. "I am asking again: do you like me? She insisted for an immediate and straight answer.

"Of course Lena; but I must tell you so far I never touched a woman with sexual intention." "I must confess I am a great admirer of your beauty," his face blushed with a tinge of shyness.

"Thank you," she said it with a romantic smile. Although no signal, of romanticism or amorousness from him, she longed to kiss him but modesty and self-pride held her back. "The first move must come from him," she told herself. So far, she had sexual intimacy with experienced men.

"Should people condemn such moves as immoral? She wondered why people make so much fuss.

"Logically speaking what is so immoral about having sex? It is physical; it is like having a meal to satisfy hunger," she would argue with her friends.

Fortunately, Krish also concurred with that opinion. He never thought of celibacy as a virtue or moral superiority.

To Lena it is a pleasant surprise as she expected Krish to react negatively, but he appeared serene and composed. He raised his voice, "I strongly believe that one must avoid carnal issues to vitiate human intellectuality."

"More importantly marriage is between two spirited human beings not just between two carnal entities." For the first time, Lena profoundly appreciated him and his sharp but manly features. She observed the glow of intellectuality in his face.

Krish's sympathetic views emboldened her; hesitated for a short while but candidly said, "Sex is an important component of happiness. It is a driving force, it is desirable, and sign of healthy living; when, where and how one enjoys sex may differ from person to person." Before he completed his sentence, she boldly affirmed her preferences.

"But personally, I am a lover of romance and I always welcome premarital sexual romance." Lena spoke plainly and suggestively.

Krish looked at Lena smilingly and expressed his reservation, "I agree with you but I prefer to wait for my first-night thrill" Lena wondered how he could impose such self-control.

"Dating is incomplete without sex" she mulled. Somehow, she had to subdue her urge to have sex with him before agreeing to marry.

However, she had to concede to accommodate Krish's feelings. "I understand your reluctance for pre-marital sex" she calmed herself.

Krish looked at Lena with some doubt. "Let me make sure. Should I intimate my parents and arrange for our marriage? Krish looked at her appealingly. He clearly spelt out he is seeking her hand in marriage, looked for a straight answer because Lena looked confused.

"Shouldn't we wait? Lena hesitated.

"What for? He questioned her.

"Sure you don't want another date? Her suggestive look did not change his mind.

"How long should we wait? She looked grumpy, expressing her disquiet. Sensing her irritability Krish tried to overdo to pacify her.

"Why can't we marry here?

"Why not have a big fat 'Indian-wedding' in India? Murli told me you also entertain such a wish." He tried to amuse Lena with another argument.

"Now that we finished our studies, we can go to India tomorrow if you wish and get married the next day" he blinked his eyes with a sparkle, as if he is acting in a drama. "I hope my parents would endorse us; they left it to my choice, anyway," he sounded assuring.

She threw an artificial smile and apparent disinterest but her voice did not conceal her concern. "What is your plan if they do not agree" she expressed her anxiety.

"I am sure they will agree with my choice." He sounded quite confident.

Thus I followed every step of their coming together. I can now recall what transpired between Krish and hisparents.

Mahesh and Parvathi came to Bombay to receive Krish at the airport and traveled together to the guest house of his company.

Krish appeared to be in a hurry, "I have to report to my boss first and join you in Delhi." After welcoming him back and a few hours rest, they raised the issue of his newfound love engagement.

"You know who that girl is – she is the socialite daughter of that termagant notorious woman, Rani of Hyderabad" Parvathi pleaded with him.

Mahesh waited a while before replying "I thought you went to America for higher studies, not in search of a bride" sarcastically quipped Maheshwar. Krish ignored his father's chiding, laughed away.

"I really liked that girl mom. She is beautiful, honest and simple person. If you meet her once - you will change your opinion"

"I want to get married to her as soon as possible," he added with great hope of endorsement from his parents.

"Are you out of your mind? Do you want to enter into a broken family?

"Besides, they are from a different caste and traditions" Parvati swiftly intervened "As far as my information goes, she is known to have entertained many 'boy friends' even as a minor girl; her best friends describe her sex-pervert," Parvati accused Lena specifically.

"You are a Brahmin boy you are our only child. Are you to renounce your *saampradaayam* (traditionality)? Mahesh tried to invoke sentimentality.

"What *saampradaayam* dad? What is so great about it? Why should we hang on to it? Krish fired a barrage of questions.

Mahesh felt challenged. "Do what you wish to do but don't blame the fundamentals of my faith. Don't ever try to blame of what you do not know. You may be President or Vice President of the world but you have no right to challenge my faith. You may not like to inherit that wisdom; but I am proud of my ancestors and I cherish that as wealth; it is beyond earthly aspects of creation, it is beyond the analytical power of all intellectuals put together. We worship this cosmic intelligence, which exists in every creature moving, non-moving, perceptible or imperceptible. We worship the whole and soul of dimensionless spirit called God" Mahesh spoke like a man possessed.

"For your information, this *Sanatana Dharma* (ancient wisdom) is the wealth of entire humanity, not just Brahmins or Hindus as you imagined. If you do not want to cherish this heritage, it is your misfortune."

"I did not expect this from a scientist, Dad! Krish mocked at his father.

In fact, Mahesh is a high-level national scientist working for DRDL (Defense Research and Development Laboratories) of India.

"I have more scientific background than you have. Despite all the scientific knowledge of modern times, I accept the unique knowledge bank in *Vedas*. Do not tell me that I am superstitious ignoramus" Mahesh appeared shaking in a fit of anger.

Krish looked distraught, dazed but appeared decisive. "Since I decided to marry her you have no right to project that she is a whore. She is honest and truthful, informed me of her previous dates but that was before we agreed for marriage. In any case, I don't mind her previous history" Krish spoke brusquely; rejected their allegation.

Hurt by his son's open defiance Mahesh got up, walked away in a huff while shouting loudly, "No one can erase your destiny, even the God cannot." He walked out to the exit gate without waiting for his wife.

Parvathi rushed out to join him "Be more discerning, that's all I am asking you," she said while walking away, wiping her tears with the sari end.

Krish begged them to stay back and listen to him. Tried to reason out, but they politely distanced themselves from him.

"From now on, you are on your own" Mahesh and Parvati left him in haste.

Almost immediately after his parents exit, he rang Lena "Get ready for a Registered marriage." "Ask your dad to arrange for marriage reception in Hyderabad." "My parents refuse to accept our wedding, but it does not matter; I know they will come around." Lena appreciated Krish's commitment.

I must also tell you how Vinay tried to break Krish's association with Lena much before the proposed marriage.

Vinay tried to discourage Krish by making some disparaging comments about Lena. Having heard that Krish will be getting married to Lena, Vinay got jealous.

As I said before, Krish met Vinay and me in New York a few years back. At that time he was totally unaware of Lena's antecedents. Incidentally, it so happened that I hade to live in NY on project work of TCS.

"I never thought we meet again," Krish told me and Vinay (the only son of Appaji). "It is sheer coincidence" Krish expressed his joy. While studying in Ahmedabad we were not that close but in NY, we re-established friendship.

"She is Lena, a good tennis player" Vinay introduced Lena. "She is also from Hyderabad." At that time, Vinay and Lena also were students in the same New York State University.

While Krish was still studying in NYSU an interesting discussion occurred between him and Vinay; at that time he ignored it, as not of importance. He never imagined that it would profoundly affect his later life.

One day Vinay saw Lena in Krish's company, wanted to talk to him, but waited until Lena left him. Vinay came running behind Krish and enquired pointedly "How much you know about this girl?

Krish looked at Vinay vaguely. Vinay came close to him and said, "She was my date until last month" he appeared aggrieved and conniving.

Krish looked at him innocently and asked, "Why are you telling me?

"It looked as though you both are getting closer - that is why" "I saw you both playing tennis on the campus," he continued, looked around like a suspicious person.

Krish appeared confused but managed to bring up a smile, commented politely "I have nothing to do with her at 'that level'. She is just a tennis partner – that's all." He laughed it away. Vinay tried to extend his enquiry.

"She is not a good girl – I am sorry to say that" he guarded his words. Vinay appeared cantankerous because he had strained relationship with his 'girl friend'. Lena rejected him since a few weeks.

"It is hard to satisfy her in the bed" he wanted to tell; but he found Krish is in no amorous mood to think of Lena as a lover. Krish shrugged-off Vinay's words.

However, he wanted to say, "It is impossible not to notice the awesome beauty of Lena" "She is a good-looking and voluptuous girl," but modesty inhibited him to vocalize.

But he noticed that many men were seeking her company; he also witnessed Lena passionately kissing an Afro-American man.

"Isn't she in love with some American man? Krish casually enquired. "Yeah she is in love with so many" Vinay replied in a complaining tone.

"She is constantly in search of ram-like Rambo; ready to sleep with anyone who appears to have those features" Vinay wanted to say it loudly but lacked guts. Vinay's body language clearly reflected his disappointment, envy, jealousy and anger.

Vinay suddenly raised his voice "She is no virgin, I know, because I made love to her." He blabbered and boasting

"Vinay is half-man" Lena told me without any reservation. She unhesitatingly rejected Vinay.

However it did not take long for the differences between Krish and Lena surfaced. Despite Krish's accommodative spirit Lena appeared quite indifferent to her husband. I witnessed Lena flaring up in a get-together party.

What happened could remain a non-issue but for Lena's animated lecture on women's rights to non-suspecting guests attending the dinner party. I heard her 'lecturing'; she began her argumentative talk by addressing men.

"Why you guys don't bring your wives for the dinner party? Would they become whores if they drink a glass of wine like the one you do? Lena embarrassed friends and relatives of Krish. Then she turned to the women "Your men can drink and dance with other women but wives are prohibited from drinking or dancing with other men." I noticed her friends sitting and chatting suddenly became silent and sullen facing the tirade of Lena.

One of the guests was provoked and her discomfiture shown in her distraught face, posed a counter question. "Why do you want us to do wrong things, Lena?

"Who defined the wrong doing, tell me" Lena pushed her head forward, retorted with a serious question. "If your husband drinks it becomes right; but if you do, it becomes wrong. Is that your definition? Is it right? She looked at them with an irritated face.

One of them retorted sternly. "No Lena, drinking by anyone and everyone is wrong. No one supports drinking"

"Is that so? I have not seen any one of you objecting your husband's sipping some whisky, I guess you are scared" she remarked sarcastically.

"That is nonsense. That is a personal choice, but who would want to do a wrong thing," another lady friend explained. Leena got up from her chair, came close to her challenger, looked intensely at her and asked, "Imagine the scene the other way.... let us assume you are seen sipping some whisky your husband sitting and watching you but does not drink - then what would you expect to happen?

"Natural reaction is to stop me from doing that wrong thing"

"Then why didn't you do the same to your husband ...now?

"He will get his punishment in the bed," another challenger laughed loudly. "But why waiting until then?

"I do not want to scold him in front of others"

"No madam. You are afraid of the imaginary consequences, and that is what we as women should not allow." "I am afraid we are allowing one set of rules for the men and one for ourselves. That is discriminatory" "And that we should stop" she emphasized that point by banging the table with her fist.

"She is a mad cow" a friend of mine rudely commented later.

"She claims she is a feminist without knowing the real background of feminist movement." "Feminism in the early 20th century is meant to mend the ways of British male chauvinists. It was for the sake of mistresses of the English men. In the context of Indian culture, the title Mistress (Mrs) is a 'Keep' (a woman solely meant to provide sexual gratification to the possessor, the man). In our culture, Shrimati is the title of a married woman. She is a legitimate, consummated married woman. She will be wholly and squarely owe all responsibility of the family without any reservation.

"Feminism in India is a borrowed idea like the Valentine day," exclaimed another friend.

Nevertheless, Lena continued her feminist talk. "Indian women continue to suffer oppression by the social scheme of things." She declared that the fight must go on. "I fear none and I am capable of acting in spite of resistance," her resolute face revealed it all.

"Women's Lib is not for negotiation," she declared in front of her husband and his relatives.

"All are equal – period. Do not discuss" was her terse message.

"If a woman laughs loudly it is manner less. If a man does it, he is authoritative. If a woman talks freely with a man, she is 'loose'. Why should you allow this to perpetrate? Lena passionately questioned her critics.

"Men can make a woman pregnant. They can't become pregnant," a man from the audience shouted at her.

"Thank God for it. If men had that ability, they could have become monstrous man-eaters."

"Seriously, if a woman can bear nine months of pregnancy, can't a man take few hours a day to give her the requisite rest? Should you ignore what you can do, such as taking care of the baby, cook food, wash dishes, make beds, settle clothes in the wardrobes etc."

"How many jobs do you expect a man to do to please his partner? The man in crowd tried to ridicule.

"Women are doing many more jobs, as wife, householder, mother, daughter-in law etc. just to keep the family going? Mostly relegated to unpaid jobs such as household choirs, and care of family, are they destined to depend on man's patronage? Is she meant for unpaid thankless jobs? Should she be kept imprisoned in the 'cages' of bodily comfort? That is utter nonsense. Equality of all must be our aim."

Lena's vociferous argument shook the entire family out of their wits. "Haven't you heard '*matrudevobhava*'? Krish's cousin tried to add sentiment.

"What do you think it means" counter question posed by Lena embarrassed the questioner. "It emphasizes that mother is God." "How many of you really consider mother is god-manifest? She had a searching look at the group; very few dared to speak as most kept silent.

"Mere rhetoric is an exaggeration of the reality. As long as she remains serving your needs she is a good mother. The moment she demands freedom she becomes bad" Lena's cynical talk is beyond the taste of householders that gathered there.

Murli continued his narration. I know Lena's childhood is one of neglect, loneliness devoid of maternal love. But I preferred to keep off that discussion.

"She lost her mind," one of our friend's wives gestured her desperation. But a lady came to her rescue. "What sort of society are we; if a woman's husband dies, she would be stripped of her personal status. They break her *gajulu* (bangles), wipe her *bottu* (beauty mark on the forehead) and make-up forbidden, wear white sarees only, and eat one meal a day and kept homebound. In some parts of our country, they used to tie the woman to dead husband's body; burn her live (*Sati*). But, if a wife dies man can happily remarry. Where are human rights? An unmarried woman, nearly forty years old, fiercely defended Lena.

I broadly agree with most of her views, but this party is not an appropriate platform for such discussions, I thought of telling Lena and the audience. In our tribal society, we do not allow such archaic practices. If a woman's husband dies, she could remarry.

I began understanding Krish's distress. He appeared embarrassed; his mother Parvathi who came there turned her head away avoiding showing her disgust. She bent her head disbelieving the happenings in her presence.

Suddenly everyone became silent. After a few moments, Parvathi appeared impatient, forced herself to speak and raised her voice. "Now let me ask you a question. Imagine you are running an office managing an estate of a million per year_ don't you need someone to look after the money? Wont you need someone to manage such an estate"? Do you expect that manager to have the same level of independence as the person fetching that kind of money? Is it not necessary for managers (man or woman) to be submissive to the person who brings that much money?

"Similarly a person earning, let's say a million bucks per year expects his or her partner to manage the means and keep up the family's wellbeing. If he or she does not assume such leadership, the family will fall apart. Leave alone the other family matters needing a lot of understanding, cohesiveness and unity. Mutual dependence, trust and sacrifice make family bonds become stronger."

"'Independence' is not what one expects out of familial relationships and wedlock," She emphasized. "Mutual dependence, security and stability are what we expect from marriage. Quality of human relationships depends upon mutual respect, courtesy and obedience," Parvati appeared irritated.

"I am not specifically targeting anyone aunty" Lena played a sympathy card, tried to take a cover, hesitated to argue with her mother-in-law Parvathi.

After bidding good night to all the friends leaving their house, I understood from Krish that he tried to reason it out with Lena.

"Don't you think you exceeded your limits" Krish looked at his wife rather unkindly.

"No I don't think so. I have every right to speak up my mind. I have nothing but woman's welfare in mind and in any case I haven't asked your advice Krish." He looked at Lena with utter contempt and disregard.

"Don't allow your tongue to rule your mind. How could you make such insensitive and callous remarks against our friends?

"It is none of your business Krish. As I was telling them, it is a conspiracy to keep people like us in silent suffocation." "I am dedicated to champion the cause of women. If you have any objection to it, let me know, I am ready to divorce you" Lena has expressed no remorse, appeared in no penitent mood. The D-word came out of Lena's mouth for the first time.

Krish remained shell-shocked. "Aren't you overdoing Lena?

"No I am not. In fact, I am tolerating a lot. Now it is time to quits." She rushed into the bath room slammed the door with a thud. Krish stood there listless called her to come out and talk to him. "You and I have nothing in common." Just when they were heatedly arguing, Murli barged in. He found Krish sitting alone in the sofa holding his head in his hands appeared sad and grim.

"Our honeymoon is over Murli," looking at his friend Krish nearly cried in an emotional outburst.

I noticed his adorable, everlasting smile wiped away from his face; his calm and collective stance disappeared. I noticed humiliation and irreconcilable anger in his body language.

Murli raised the level of our curiosity. Let me come back to the background story, the way in which destiny brought these two together, despite so many hurdles.

Ramlu always feared if Lena would walk in the shoes of her mother Rani.

Actually I did not expect that Krish's marriage with Lena would go smoothly; but for my uncle's passionate belief in Hindu traditions. Murli continued after he ensured that we were keenly following him.

Uncle Ramlu did not leave things go astray; he vowed to bring rapproachment between Krish and his parents.

After listening to Krish and Lena's plans to go ahead without the approval of Krish's parents, he got angry and took the next available flight to Delhi to meet with Mahesh and Parvathi.

As soon as he reached Delhi, Ramlu rang Mahesh; he sensed that Parvathi and Mahesh sounded very positive and courteous.

He rang Lena "Let me tell you, Mahesh invited me for dinner in their house this evening. No ill will at all," Lena noticed the relief in his voice.

Ramlu took his Telugu Brahmin friend and his wife to give them a big silver tray with flowers, fruits and unstitched clothes (saree and dhoti); turmeric and kumkum (bottu) in separate ornate silver containers. "Keep that in the car" Ramlu requested his friend.

Mahesh and Parvati appeared very cordial in receiving Ramlu and his friends.

Looking at their modest house, Ramlu said, "This house now might fetch you a minimum of 3 or 4 crores" Mahesh chuckled with a hint of exaggeration.

"I worked in Delhi for three years and searched for a decent sized place, I found the prices were abominably high. I could not afford an apartment, let alone independent house," he told Mahesh. "I know how expensive Delhi became." "Before retirement, I worked as Joint Secretary in the Ministry of Finance. A big builder of Delhi offered me a fully furnished and designed villa if I could do some favor in return. He did not realize he is talking to a wrong person" he paused a moment, and said, "Am I boring you with self dubba (self praise)," Ramlu looked self-effacing.

"No, you are not boring; what you said is absolutely right." Mahesh added "I could not afford and I had to buy this M I G House in far-off Mayur Vihar. Now it is in demand but a few decades ago it was very cheap."

While talking he walked around appreciating the surrounds of Mayur Vihar house "You did the right thing in buying your own house in Delhi" Ramlu said while sitting on the sofa; started praising him in front of his friends. "Mahesh is a dedicated Scientist, and a great asset to our country. He declined US offer and came back to serve here. He is a true patriot" Ramlu's compliment embarrassed Mahesh. His friend kept nodding his head in apparent appreciation of Ramlu's comments. Mahesh kept himself busy with cleaning the table and shuffling the coffee cups in a tray.

"Ever since you left Hyderabad I lost touch with you; I did not know your whereabouts. As I said many times before 'I sincerely apologize my wife's indecent and rude behavior. Although it was a long time back episode, I remember how indecently Rani behaved. I beg you to forgive me. You must know we are not living together," Ramlu's twisted facials and eyebrows conveyed his resentment of Rani.

He took a big breath, folded his hands and said, "Don't keep that incident in mind. Accept my daughter as your daughter. Krish is in love with Lena – please bless them, forgive their ineptitude" Ramlu virtually begged them with all humility and humbleness.

"Without your presence I will not allow the marriage to proceed." His friends joined him "Please join him in his return flight; he booked tickets for you both."

Mahesh looked at Parvati "My son Krish may not like us to attend" peeved and frustrated Mahesh and Parvati muttered, but appeared softening their stand.

"Forget all that entirely, sir. It is time to forgive their immature behavior" Ramlu offered a plank to reconcile.

"I grew among Brahmin families. I never stopped admiring their life styles." Mahesh observed the relish with which Ramlu ate various items of the food Parvathi made.

While they were talking and enjoying the rice pudding, doorbell rang, Parvathi went up to answer only to find Krish at the doorstep. Parvathi couldn't control her emotion embraced him, while everyone got up and jubilantly welcomed him.

"How did you come at this late hour? Mahesh asked his son while looking at his watch; it showed ten in the night.

"My boss took a chartered flight and I joined him. We will go back to Bombay by early hours of tomorrow." Krish bent and touched his parents' feet. Mahesh embraced and blessed his son.

"Dad, Mom, I cannot go through the marriage without you" Krish's anguish was obvious. "Forgive my ignorance Dad. I did not mean to hurt you. I got carried away by my arrogance. Don't mind that Dad, please" tears shined in his eyes.

Mahesh took his arm around his waist drew him closer "I know you valued your parents very high, otherwise you could have gotten married in NY without telling us" Mahesh commented in a reconciliation mood. Father and son's interaction pleased Parvathi.

Ramlu wiped his eyes and said, "I am so pleased" choked with emotion he could hardly spell out those words from his mouth. His friend Sastry silently walked out to the car brought the silver tray. Ramlu signaled Sastry and his wife to hand over the clothes, ornaments along with the tray.

"These are modern times, we don't need to be so formal" Parvathi received the tray and placed it before their family deity Lord Venkateswara.

"I am sorry my wife is not here with me as she is not living with me" Ramlu expressed his regret.

"Not a worry in the world sir" Mahesh shook his hands. Ramlu pointed the accompanying couple and said "They are my best friends."

"I know them for many years. Sastry and his wife Lakshmi are well-known Telugu persons in Delhi, and they are known for their kindness, compassion and charity. You chose the right people" Mahesh complimented.

Krish curiously watched the proceedings. Parvathi applied kumkum (red powder) on his forehead and asked him to wrap the new dhoti presented by his would-be father-in-law around his waist. Krish appeared disinclined. "It is important to observe this betrothal formality" Parvathi insisted. He obeyed her order.

"I miss my mom's home food, that's why I came home. I didn't know uncle Ramlu came here." Krish knew his mom would fall for his praise. Sastry's wife added "My son and his American born Punjabi girl do not entertain any of our culture; have no idea of Telugu Bhojanam (Telugu meals). Thank God there are boys like Krishna, still loving mom's food." Neither Parvathi nor Mahesh know that their son eats everything that moves on earth. Krish looked at his watch and hurried his mother to give him some food to eat.

"I have to be at Hyatt by twelve midnight" he rushed himself to the dining room. Mahesh excused Ramlu and his friends and sat alongside Krish at the dining table.

"Dad, my boss will be attending the marriage," Krish boasted; Maheshwar tapped him on his shoulder as sign of his pride, "Isnt he German? Mahesh knew the bigwigs of various international companies.

"Keep up the good work. Hard work is the basis of success," Mahesh acknowledged his achievement.

"My boss chose me to go to Boston for a difficult negotiation" Krish tried to impress his father.

"I know you can do it." Mahesh looked at him with pride. Suddenly he appeared solemn "I will pay for your honeymoon in Shimla." "Me and my friend Satpal, will make all the arrangements in Shimla. I will bring the air tickets with me to Hyderabad."

"That's great Dad, I appreciate that. I am sure Lena appreciates more." "We have less than a week before marriage."

"I have to be in Bangkok tomorrow night and Pattaya for two days. Time is short, Dad."

"Let him eat his meal peacefully, first eating and then talking," Parvathi warned Mahesh not to disturb him while eating. She appeared pleased watching her son eating the food with great relish.

"Hope you find time to marry my daughter" Ramlu joked followed by a loud laughter by everyone. "I will fly a million miles to reach her hand in time" Krish affectionately shook

Sastry's hands. "I will locate your son in Boston if at all I go again to US," Krish promised Sastry.

Ramlu took Krish's parents along with him to Hyderabad.

A few weeks after the wedding was over, I visited him as a matter of routine courtesy and stragely I found Krish in great anguish.

"What happened to you Krish? I tried to share his grief.

"She is impossible Murli" hardly audible words came out of his mouth.

"What is happening Krish" I anxiously asked him.

"Without any provocation, she argued if a married man could have sex with other women, why not married women have sex with other men? I then asked her "Would you do that? She shot a reply forthwith, "If my sex needs are not met I will do that. What's wrong with that", she slapped an answer? Repeating what she said Krish sounded disgusted. He rang his mother if she could help.

I pitied him for he knows not that Lena is a misinformed, self-opinioned hardcore activist for women's liberty and equal rights.

"That crazy girl can make such bold and inappropriate statements" I joined him in condemning her; but I also know how rude she could become. I tried to comfort him with some fill-words, "Don't mind her Krish, she does not mean any of it; believe me" I tried to mollify his feelings.

Few minutes later, his mother Parvathi entered the house. She looked around and asked, "Is she home? Hastily went inside.

"No mom, she is angry with me as usual and locked herself in the bath" he appeared languid slumped into a chair. Parvathi came close to her son placed her hand on his head "why so much fuss? She appeared sympathetic but certainly agitated.

"I expected this Krish," she mumbled while caressing Krish.

"I don't know what to do mom." He explained the gist of their verbal duel. Lena was peeping at us from the half-opened bathroom.

"You do nothing. I take care to talk to Lena, she is a good girl," she climbed the stairs. Just then, Lena went back into her room silently after listening to their conversation in secret.

"Come in aunty" Lena greeted her getting up from the edge of the bed. "Sit you Lena" Parvathi sat beside her and took her both hands into hers.

"Look my child, life is not black and white; there are many shades in between. My advice to you both is not to hurt yourselves because of some XYZ's issues. I fully agree with you on matters of women's welfare." Lena looked at her with cynicism. Parvathi sensed her disbelief.

"I will certainly encourage Krish to share your views. But, who am I to tell? You both are very intelligent, educated and in any case, Krish is very sensitive to women's welfare. He has tremendous interest in public affairs, I guess you can convince each other and reach consensus by arguing on facts and not imaginations. I can tell you negativism is not a useful tool to convey your ideas to someone else. Be positive and be active, but offer solutions, not repeated narration of problems" Lena patiently heard her mother-in-law.

"Krish takes everything lightheartedly; he evades answering me. His has the last word on everything. He pays no attention to my concerns aunty," Lena continued in her glum and gloom. Parvathi tried to convince her but found Lena obstinate and indifferent. Parvathi made efforts to calm down Lena's uncompromising attitude.

"I tell you – let Krish try out taking up posting in Boston, USA; that will iron him flat, make him a better person. All his evasiveness disappears." Parvathi's artificial smile signaled the depth of her disquiet. But she had no idea of the 'real' problem, appeared totally unaware of Krish's impotence problem.

Lena laughed philosophically at Parvathi's gag comment. "I wish you are right." In any case, her skepticism and apathy towards her mentors is a feature of Lena's style of living. Disbelief and suspicion encroach into every act she engages in, therefore hesitated to respond positively to her mother-in-law's suggestion.

Parvathi knew that Lena is not only a pampered child but uncultivated to family life. "She certainly is a bad cookie," she told herself. Lena showed no signs of meltdown.

At that stage I noticed the fissures between them were widening.

"Divorce him," shouted Rani despite the fact that marriage took place. Rani demanded that the marriage nullified. I recollect the fiery war of words between Rani and Ramlu.

As Rani did not like Ramlu getting closer to Krish's parents she shouted, "Brahmins are racists," Rani shouted. "They find fault with everything the Non-Brahmins do."

"Is it because they asked you to remove shoes before entering their house? Ramlu confronted her headlong.

"They think they are the custodians of our culture. They are so arrogant and rude to me," she emphasized on every word she uttered. Contempt spewed out of her eyes.

"No, they are not. They are very polite –you are the one that flared up there and left their house in a huff."

"Shut your mouth Ramlu. I am not expecting you to support me. You never can understand me," she pushed her husband in a surge of uncontrolled anger. Ramlu nearly fell on the ground but managed to hold on to the edge of dinner table and withstood the push.

"You are indecent, discourteous and utterly rude" he got up in fury and yelled at her at the top of his voice.

"Calm down uncle" I urged my uncle. "How can I ignore this? She is the spoiling the marriage of her daughter just because of her ego. Nothing else" Ramlu shouted with anger. He sat down in the sofa at my behest but appeared profusely sweating and red-faced.

Rani left the house ranting and panting.

"She is irresponsible, arrogant and self obsessed foolish woman. Stupid woman, she cannot understand the sophistication of Krish and his parents. They are extremely polite and polished people. You rarely meet such people."

Standing on the other side of the fence, Rani shouted angrily, "That son of a peon has neither self-esteem nor respect for his wife. I gave him a lift in life. If I had not married him, he would have remained a clerk in my dad's office. I picked him up, heaped praise on him before my dad and married him despite my dad's doubts. He is an ungrateful, uncouth son of a bitch. He showed his real colors only after marrying me. In the name of duty and *dharma* he had developed the guts to criticize my father, his benefactor. He accused my father of corruption and nepotism."

"He belongs to gutter-culture; I should not have picked him up. He does not know how to keep up his status. To make my life miserable he wants me to descend to his level of low caste slavishness" Rani shot her words recklessly.

We heard Murli's narration about their disharmony with rapt attention. What we could not understand was how Ramlu got married to such hotheaded woman Rani.

He smiled at us saying "Destiny sir, destiny"; he continued again.

In fact, Rani's father selected Ramlu as a groom for his darling daughter, not only based on his caste but his education, a degree holder. Rani's father Danny feared the sexual precocity of his daughter; and failed love affairs prompted him to act quickly.

Rani refused to settle for less, she desired an obedient husband. Her eerie sense, that Ramlu is not just a good-looking person belonging to their caste but educated, ambitious and hardworking. That was her reason to get close to him.

"Neither pity nor sympathy, it is pure and simple self interest" I was told. Actually, Ramlu was working in the District Court, as a Bench-clerk before his selection to IAS. Nevertheless, he worked hard and succeeded in getting IAS selection.

"I owe my job selection to my tribal belonging," I heard him saying this to his friends. "I agreed to marry Rani because she was good-looking and attractive, but not because she is the daughter of District Judge" he denigrated the claim of any patronage. "No pity, nor sympathy - it is pure and simple self-interest" he repeated that opinion many times before falling out with Rani.

In fact me and Ramlu owe our success to Dr Ambedkar. Hence he did not hesitate to tell everyone "I am ever grateful to Dr Ambedkar for the proviso for Reservations to ST and SC candidates." "If there was no such provision in the constitution I would not have been in IAS, my performance was never optimal.

Besides, uncle Ramlu always admitted "I am a self-made man." I know uncle never allowed false pride, "I am the son of a Peon and I grew in the ambience of poverty and squalor. I cannot forget that. That is the reason why I never claim any privilege of office when I am out of office hours or leave office for private reasons."

But aunty Rani always wanted to misuse power and prestige of his position. All who knew him tell us that Ramlu really practiced what he believed. He remained simple and straightforward, free and fair, able and assertive in his job.

I remember uncle advising us "Corruption is corrosive; it evokes injustice, inefficiency, deny progressivism and deprive people of their privileges."

In fact, I myself have on one occasion tried to take the side of a false claim and took representation to the Collector on behalf of false claimants. He pulled me up and chided me misusing caste-card to intimidate a legitimate upper caste owner of a piece of land. "It is gross violation of constitutional guarantees. I will not allow this. I know you came to me with the support of an MP (Member of Parliament) of our caste – but, it won't work," he asserted, asked us to leave the office immediately. He is such an upright man.

I can tell you about Rani's family, the old-time story narrated by my mother about Rani aunty's father Danny, Ramlu and other people of our caste, Murli looked at our sad faces and continued.

When I was young my family were desperately poor while Rani's family was doing well in life. Rani's family are snobbish; they never allowed us to enter their home. My mother and grandmother told me many bitter stories about Danny and Rani. My grandma's age was more than ninety years, but her memory was impeccable although she was occasionally babbling something unintelligent in between.

Let me narrate their story in their own words.

"You know Rani's father Danny was the son of a Sepoy of British army. His father lost his life fighting for the British in the First World War, died somewhere in a foreign country. The then government gave his son, the lone survivor of the Sepoy a chance to acquire English education, as a compensation for the loss of his father in the war. Danny smartly managed to climb up in life but developed arrogance, became utterly snobbish."

"Despite his efforts to mix only with forward caste people, (but those days were different), there were not many who would allow Danny to blend with them. I know he always had grouse against forward cast people. A kind of segregation frustrated him."

"He rose to the height of District Magistrate, but he became corrupt and did a lot of injustice to his own family. We resented his selfish behavior."

"Danny abandoned his first wife because she was black and illiterate, managed to get married to an Anglo-Indian girl. He converted himself into Christianity, but later changed to his Tribal Hinduism after the death of his Anglo-Indian wife. That woman died young and ever since he remained unmarried."

But, I was told that he had several women friends for his sexual needs, I chuckled.

"He was a known womanizer," my mother used to point out.

"Any how I must tell you I rescued his daughter from many awkward situations. I even neglected my own infant child to breast-fed Rani, looked after her because she was a motherless child of our Danny. Nevertheless, Rani turned out to be a replica of her father, developed arrogance because she was fair complexioned and educated. She became so snobbish that, that ungrateful woman referred me as her servant to her rich friends."

"Because I am black, less privileged and from poor community she would not treat me equally. From then on I distanced myself from Rani; she never bothered to contact me either." My mother sounded equally indignant, indifferent and unconcerned.

However, my own life-story is no different. Although under-privileged and destitute, Luck favoured me, Ramlu took great interest in me, educated and inspired me to work hard. It is because of him I achieved IIM (Indian Institute of Management) qualification.

As i told you before, Uncle Ramlu is a great admirer of Balasaheb Ambedkar, Chairman of Republic of India's Constitution Assembly that framed our egalitarian constitution.

"Thanks to our great leader and visionary Ambedkar we are getting the benefits of free India as we are positively discriminated. However, we must make good use of Reservation policy and constitutional guarantee. Even if you do not perform well in the competitive exam you still can get better opportunities. You should aim at the highest" uncle Ramlu's continuous encouragement led me to have a positive outlook.

Therefore, I owe a lot to him. Since I had no one else to look for, I connected myself to Aunty Rani, my maternal uncle's cousin-daughter and her husband Ramlu. Rani outrightly rejected me, never respected me as equal to them; however, I never bothered to give any importance to her hysterics.

After many years of unhappy marriage, aunty Rani left her husband finally. She demanded seperate accomodation in the same compound, independent from her husband.

Discord and dissent were features of Rani and Ramlu. Rani never stopped complaining Ramlu conspired with the Brahmin family to wean away Lena from her. "He did many such spiteful things," claimed Rani. She never stopped accusing her estranged husband of all evils. She despised him intensely "Ramlu is a nasty person, he even manhandled me," she kept complaining.

"She deserves it" many in our family commented. However, Ramlu continued to deny her accusations. "She is conceited arrogant cheat. If there is God he should paralyze her tongue," he cursed her in my presence.

"This self-obsessed woman does not care who gets sacrificed" he fumed with anger. "She cares little about Lena's future. How can she hate Krish, a lovable boy, just because he is a Brahmin? His fury and frustration were getting worse, I thought; certainly affected his health.

I was afraid of his health. I warned him many times. "You are oversensitive if I may say so. Your anger may harm you.

The other day you nearly got heart attack – you remember"
I cajoled him. I saw him virtually panting, sweating and
shaking with uncontrolled anger.

He vehemently pleaded "No Murli you guys may not
understand the implications of such behavior from her. I
must shut her foul mouth."

Ramlu's deteriorating health brought me closer to him.

I do not remember exactly when but it was a few weeks after
his daughter's marriage - he really got worse. I was alone
watching him.

Not knowing what was happening jubilant Krish entered
Ramlu's house. I signaled Krish to observe low voice as
Ramlu appeared sleepy after a short but mean fighting with
his wife Rani. I took Krish to an adjacent room, explained
the reason for Ramlu's exhaustion.

"Crisis? Krish lightheartedly asked. I understood Krish had
come to convey some information.

"What is up Krish? I whispered after sitting close to him.
Krish silently pointed his fingers at Ramlu and gestured his
need for rest. I told him of all the happenings.

"I gradually mellowed him down after he had a serious tiff
with Aunty." "Nothing new Krish, it was Raniji's routine.
Cursing her husband is her pastime" I feigned a smile.

"Poor uncle he had to put up with this kind of harassment at this late age" Krish's sympathy oozed out for him. We could hear Ramlu's snoring like a lion roaring.

Krish could not control his happiness. In child-like voice and gesture, he expressed immense joy "For the time being Lena did not raise the issue of divorce."

"What about Boston posting? Did she really agree to accompany you to Boston," I asked him excitedly. "Yes, yes" short but sharp answer from Krish gladdened me. I looked at uncle piteously. He appeared passive and peaceful, snoring away his woes. "As soon as he wakes up we will tell him this good news" I looked at Krish assuring.

"He appears pale" Krish closely watched Ramlu and commented anxiously, I also looked at him closely and found him conscious but not able to speak. Saliva drooling out of the corner of his mouth he appeared terribly ill. "He appears ill - terribly ill" he shouted. We rushed him to the hospital and rang his doctor-friend, urging him to come immediately to follow the ambulance.

Within a few minutes, the doctor arrived, diagnosed Brain Stroke and took him to the hospital. Except Rani everyone else reached hospital to see Ramlu. Lena cried in silence, as she knew what caused his uncontrolled anger.

Lena looked at her father, kissed his hand affectionately and assured him. "Don't worry about me, dad. I really love Krish – no one can separate me from him." Ramlu cried, wanted to say something but could not. Nurse rushed into the room requested visitors to exercise some restraint.

"His condition is fragile – please avoid emotional surges."

"How is your dad? Rani casually made a cursory inquiry.

"You don't come near here mom. I want him to live" Lena snubbed her, showed no courtesy.

"I have nothing to do with him. I have neither ill will nor good will. I am living on my own. He does not need me nor do I. I don't care even you - if that comes to that." Her antics appeared rude, uncivilized and cruel.

Lena found her mother's attitude unacceptable, but could not vocalize. "Lived together for 30 years, but appeared completely unconcerned, no sentiment." She appeared utterly shocked and dejected.

"But why do people behave like this" was her mute inquiry.

"May be self-obsession, super-ego and attitude of humiliating others" she mulled.

"You are no less danger. Your Feminism is an excuse to show off your edge over your husband. But if you continue like your mother, you may soon fear your own image," an inner voice echoed.

"None should suffer the fate of my father," she told herself.

Krish observed Lena calm down after all the fuss and fury of her mother.

Later, Krish accompanied by Lena visited him in the hospital to convey the news of his posting in Boston. "I am glad Lena agreed to accompany you," were the first few cohesive words that came out of his mouth.

"But, Krish, make sure you remove her from the influence of her mother. That devil might brain-wash her." I noticed Ramlu's annoyance.

"You don't worry uncle; I will take care of Lena. Ramlu's body language is one of less fear and more confidence. "I don't care what happens to me - my darling daughter should be free from marital problems. I know how painful it could become," he told me.

Uncle Ramlu looked at me and said, "In fact I pursued this Brahmin boy as Lena's groom, with your active help. My reasons were - Brahmins are simple and they are more sentimental, they remain loyal. No matter what anybody says, Brahmins are compassionate and considerate."

"I am glad you kept protecting me, against onslaughts of Rani. I genuinely believe Rani is a bad influence on Lena." He fumbled for words but managed to convey his feelings. He appeared emotionally fragile as he looked at me with tear-filled eyes.

I affectionately placed my hand on his shoulder, took his normal hand and gestured my gratitude. He drew my hand close to his chest and said, "I owe you a lot."

"Do not think of that uncle," I gestured him to keep calm. I once again recollected the cause for their conflict.

Poor Raniji - none of her grandiose ideas worked. She once told Ramlu "Our Tribal Welfare Minister's son Abhay is willing to marry Lena."

"That bastard's son, no way" shouted Ramlu. "I know both father and son are drug peddlers. I read a report that they cultivate Ganja on the high mountains."

"How dare you accuse such nice people" Rani fired at Ramlu.

"Go and lick their bums if you like, but don't ask me or my daughter to do that" he retorted harshly.

"I won't allow ordinary fellows like your nephew or any such fellows, to go anywhere near my daughter, not even her shadow." She emphasized the words 'my daughter'.

"When did she become 'your daughter'? Ramlu looked at her face with contempt.

I wondered why they are fighting between themselves because I know Lena would out rightly reject their fancy ideas. I knew for sure Lena would have her own say. She told me many times before that 'marriage is individuals' choice, purely personal affair, parents are for endorsing'.

Anyhow, I asked Raniji not to worry about my involvement; Lena wants to marry someone of her choice, who understands her feminist ideas and free life style. I know Lena has her own ideas. She is not going to be won over by ideas of a fellow like me. But Raniji thinks I am a bad influence.

I remembered, many times in the past, I had to restrain and urge Uncle to keep cool, as he is physically getting weaker and fragile.

Ramlu partially recovered after the stroke he suffered during his wordy duel with Rani –but he regained most of his hand movements and speech within a short span of time. The first few words he spoke although disjointed, were about Lena.

"Make marriage once-a-lifetime affair. Be wedded forever. Grant me a grandchild. That is all I need, nothing else from you guys." He broke down sobbing with words bursting out in short spells. I tried to decipher what he wanted to get across, while trying to console him. Lena affectionately drew him closer, hugged him, tears rolling out.

"Don't worry about me" he turned his head to the other side, paused for brief moments, continued. "I am glad you married Krish" Ramlu looked at Krish with a gentle smile and asked me to drag his chair near to his bed. Krish dragged his chair closer, sat on the edge of the chair showed enthusiasm to the father-daughter dialogue.

Ramlu recalled the past, "Frankly speaking, my childhood was an epitome of misery as I hail from a downtrodden family of illiterate tribes.

"In my college days, I grew in the house of my guru Somayajulu and later in life worked closely with Sarma, a dedicated teacher. Both Brahmin families treated me very well. Until Rani entered my life, I never knew harsh words or rude behavior." "After those golden days were over, misery wrapped me within its long arms."

"I must say I married trouble in the shape of Rani. She became my daily dose of suffocation. She must have had sadistic pleasure by tormenting me" he paused and looked at Lena. "Somehow, your mom disliked my honesty and self-restraint. She wanted to misuse my office and I had to stop her. She hated me for that. She enjoyed teasing me, relentlessly harassed me with all sorts of accusations. In her wild imaginations, I am her enemy. She says that I ruined her life. She ridiculed my dedication to work and zero-tolerance for corruption as a sign of weakness."

"The only good thing that happened in my life was your birth despite your mom's refusal to continue pregnancy." "She wanted termination of pregnancy, I refused consent. She became hysterical, intimidated me with the threat of suicide in protest. I remember her violent shouts, "you made me pregnant, so you take care of the baby you wanted. She refused to see you after delivery."

"Poor you – grew up in the hands of servants and housemaids (dayees) while your mom busied herself with many of her socialite friends; Murli's mother breast-fed you. She took care of you until you were six years old. I had to admit you in a boarding school. A few months after you graduated from high school, you left India for study abroad. You hardly lived with us. I regretfully admit you grew up in your own house as a guest." He took a deep breath and continued, "Now, you are all set to go to far off lands with your husband" he gazed at Lena and Krish with tear-filled eyes. Lena hugged her father.

"Sweetest moments of my life were when I was holding you as a baby. You were a ton of pleasure for me." "I know it is hard for you to remember your childhood memories: almost every day I was coming home before your sleep-time only to see your smiling face and cuddle you in my arms. Those were my most cherished rewards in life."

Lena wiped her tears "Yes dad I remember the ecstatic feeling when you were home. Yes, dad I very well remember" she mumbled. "I used to sit alone waiting for your arrival. The moment I saw you I was jumping with joy" tears rolled down Lena's cheeks. Both remained silent for a few moments. We were moved by the recollection of their past.

Ramlu suddenly changed pitch after wiping his nose. "In one aspect your mom was right. One must enjoy youthful life to the maximum. Do not compromise on that, may be money can be a cause for worry. Nevertheless, do not be bothered about money. I can tell you very confidently happiness is not within the bounds of money. In fact, 'happiness' is always elusive. Make use of right amounts of money, honey and many other things. Make your own unique formula."

He then turned his attention to Krish. "I am immensely proud of making you my son-in-law. Not only because you are handsome and brilliant but you belonged to a family of gentle people. I deeply regret the misbehavior of my wife. Her rudeness toward you and your family is condemnable. I never forgave her. But you know she is uncontrollable. He tried to get up from his bed, took both hands of Krish and said, "Forgive my failure. Forgive her arrogance and inanity."

Krish appeared moved by Ramlu's sudden gesture of acquiescence. "Uncle you should not be saying those words" he got up from his chair with utter humility, touched the hands of Ramlu with his bent head. He hugged him with affection.

"Take good care of my Lena." He took the hands of his daughter, placed them in Krish's hand, and said, "Take care of Krish. He is your friend, father and family."

Ramlu was once a high profile, upright and honest official controlling the destiny of many people, now, appeared begging a young man for forgiveness and compassion.

A profound thought ran in my mind. Since I knew how uncle Ramlu struggled to keep up the family dignity despite Rani aunty's indifference and self-obsession; it did not surprise me.

"My father is a great admirer of you, Uncle" Krish diverted the subject.

"Your dad is a great man, a typical Brahmin though. He is known for his no-nonsense attitude, a disciplined follower of rules and regulations. Nevertheless, he is a genius and a walking compendium of knowledge and his personal code of conduct exemplary. I sought his advice many a time before he was transferred from Hyderabad."

"You may not know how embarrassing it was for me due to Rani's rudeness and arrogance. It was shocking." He took a deep sigh, looked at Murli "Because of the tiff with Rani, a troubling neighbor, his father applied for transfer to Madras. I am not sure if that is true" Ramlu turned towards Krish asking in an apologetic manner.

"Past is past uncle" Krish tried to soothe his hurt. At this juncture, he turned to me.

"You know something Murli, "uncle sounded complaining seriously took my hand. He said, "Just recently Rani threatened Parvathi with dire consequences." Listening him Krish appeared taken aback, jerked forward in the chair

"Yes I know that uncle; aunty threatened Krish's mother with dire consequences if Krish agreed to marry Lena."

She insisted Lena must marry her nephew.

I pleaded with her. "Talk to Lena, convince her." She retorted saying that I am influencing her negatively. That was not all. She threatened me saying her nephew Gond Raj, will see (my end) if Lena gets married to Krish" I had to reveale that fact to Ramlu.

Ramlu showed his disdain, "When it suited, she would boast, "I come from the royal family of a Chief of Raj Gonds a tribe of Chattisgarh. Since I hail from another tribe called Parthans family, she expects me to remain as servant of the Raj Gonds."

"We the Raj Gonds do not allow this subservience and intermix. We hate mixing with plains' people," she claims. I know all Raj Gonds have lost their kingdoms under the British Raj. They all now live in miserable conditions, worse than beggars. In fact, Rani disowned relatives of her own family. All their community knows her snobbishness. Nevertheless, it was I who rescued some of them without Rani knowing.

Krish looked baffled; he knows Ramlu is a Tribal from Adilabad. But is he a Raja of Gond tribe? He later asked me if it meant something serious.

"Yes of course. Most of the erstwhile princely states of tribal belt of Andhra Pradesh, Bastar, Chattisgarh were ruled by Raj Gonds. Now, there are no more Rajas, but my sect, Parthans still perform important religious rituals for our community. I gave him a brief background of Rani and Ramlu's claim and counter claim. In fact, Ramlu and I are Pathans.

"India's cultural diversity is unfathomable." Mystified Krish made a profound comment after a long pause.

Do you wish to know Ramlu's family background? I asked Krish, looked at Krish's face if he is ready for a shocker. He appeared eager to know.

He is the son of a school attendant, in other words a peon cadre person. But, Ramlu as a child grew in the house of a Brahmin teacher. He 'adopted' Ramlu, inducted him into formal education and later sought government help to pay for his higher education. He was the one that encouraged him to take IAS exams. He tutored him very intensively and Ramlu did not disappoint him. He got selected to IAS Cadre. His first posting was in Vizag district as trainee RDO (Revenue Divisional Officer) of Narsipatnam-Chintapalli division, and subsequently rose to the District Collector's position. He had a mercurial progress in various jobs at different levels and rose to become Joint Secretary in the Ministry of Finance, New Delhi.

While your father was working there - you and your parents were neighbors to him. I guess you are still very young before they left Hyderabad"

"What about you, how close are you to your uncle, if I may ask? Krish confronted Murli's curiosity was obvious.

Initially I was taken as a servant boy in their house and later 'adopted' by uncle Ramlu against the will of aunty Rani. Aunty treated me with contempt and intense dislike. She hated every step of my progress in the school, college and IIM. In her view, I should not have been encouraged, much against the wishes of uncle Ramlu.

I had a rough time in their house. Raniji was giving hefty physical punishment for every little fault of mine. Severe manhandling and starving me were her methods. Many times, I thought of running away from home but Ramlu uncle's gentle consolation was healing my wounds instantly. I was like a boxers punch bag, back to my studies with full vigor. Uncle moved me later to a Tribal Welfare Students Hostel in Adilabad. After my graduation in business management, I was the lucky one selected to study in the prestigious Indian Institute of Management (IIM), Ahmadabad. You know the rest, as we met there in Ahmadabad during our college days and surprisingly we met again.

Krish continued in his interest to know more about the background of Lena and her parents.

"Pardon me for asking this question: how did uncle Ramlu got married to Rani if the caste difference was so important for Raniji. Was it a love marriage" Krish put an unpleasant face while making inquiry.

That is another story Krish, if you have patience to hear. I can only narrate the gist of what I heard from my elders who knew them.

Raniji's grandfather was a sepoy (soldier) in the British Army who died in action in the Second World War on the Indo-Burmese border. Since the remains of the body were not found, the Commanding Officer took special interest in the case. He found that the lone survivor of the deceased was his orphan son, a mother-less child and had none to take care.

The officer asked his Indian cook to take care of the boy and educate him under his supervision. That boy, later the father of Raniji performed well in his school, and Law College, became a Magistrate. He was given an English name Danny but his real name was Shimbu, of Gond tribe.

Since Danny grew in the household of the English man, he was thoroughly anglicized. He distanced himself from his tribal community and married an Anglo-Indian woman. Raniji is born to her. Unfortunately, her mother died at young age due to suspected suicide.

After his bitter experience with the first marriage, Danny considered re-marriage was burdensome. In any case, he was known womanizer.

"Rani must have noticed her dad's frequently changing female company since the death of her mother. Although he remained unmarried, he could not raise his daughter properly."

Uncle told me how beautiful Rani was in her younger days. "I must say Rani got the color of her mother and the physical features of Raj Gonds. Her physical features were great. She became a beautiful young lady, certainly enticed me," Ramlu admitted.

"Mind you, her physical beauty is skin deep and deceptive," Ramlu added caustic comments.

Anyhow, the household staff of Danny reared Rani since her father spared no time for her. Therefore, Rani had to learn all the malingering tactics to seek attention from her father. Although good-looking, Rani by nature is fussy and complaining type. Since my mother was a servant with them she told me her tantrums were a nightmare to the servants.

Ramlu's entry into Danny's family, seem predestined. Ramlu uncle told me "My entry into their life is predestined. I was a temporarily appointed deputy in the district court of Danny. I met Danny while he was the District Magistrate of Mehaboobnagar. In our casual conversation, we traced our Gond heritage and got closer. Danny kept watching my personality and performance."

From then on, Ramlu frequented their house not only for social reasons but also because of his attraction to Raniji. She was equally interested in dating Ramlu.

"Rani is a hooker" Ramlu joked. "I fell into her lap" and "conveyed my intention to marry her."

To Danny this was god-sent. Since he had no social contacts Ramlu's gate crashing came in handy. At that time, Ramlu was preparing for AP State's Group-1 officer and other competitive examinations under the guidance of his mentor Somyajulu. As expected, Ramlu did very well in the competitive exams. Danny promptly arranged the marriage of his daughter with Ramlu, the budding officer. And, sadly the bliss of marriage lasted only two years until Rani became pregnant with Lena.

Uncle Ramlu frequently complained "My marital life was over after our togetherness for two years, the reason was: I wanted to have children, but Rani had exactly opposite views. She refused to have babies for fear of losing her shape and charm. She accidentally became pregnant against her will."

"She demanded abortion, showed no signs of compromise. However, Danny compromised them and the pregnancy continued despite Rani's reluctance. After the birth of Lena, Rani suffered post-natal depression, neglected the child and refused to acknowledge that Ramlu is her husband. She avoided all interactions with him.

Uncle declared, "What may come, I will not divorce. My people feel ashamed if I do that" Ramlu refused to divorce her.

"I will lose my ijjat (family pride)" he told the mediators. Danny advised Rani not to go to court as it entails more complications. At last, they agreed to live under one roof but not as wife and husband. Lena left her parents to her boarding school.

"It is a shame Ramlu does not have that administrative control over his staff." Rani never allowed her husband's restraint.

Thus every instance, every interaction between them continued in the tenor of mutual disgust. "Now that they departed from each other permanently, one can describe their marriage as failed, indeed a sad saga of ego clash." I looked at Krish who appeared confused.

"Lucky, Lena grew up in a boarding school, oblivious of parents troubles. I am sure she has some idea of the ambience of hostility."

We heard Murli's narrative with rapt attention and we concluded that Ramlu must be a patient and tenacious character. Enquired if he could get hold of some old photographs.

"I guess uncle sensed that Lena is emulating her mother" Krish made a poignant comment. I observed his awkward

facial movements. I knew that Lena reluctantly agreed to follow him to Boston.

"I am doing this to keep my father happy" she showed her resentment in no uncertain words.

"Some are born to offend while some remain guilty," Krish muttered. I too felt offended at her callous remarks. I hoped Lena would realize her mistake.

Krish quipped "She may be thinking I am weak-minded. But as my mom says patience is virtue, but persistence conveys conviction."

Krish's penitence has a gross resemblance to Ramlu's predicament. Disgusted with Lena he expressed, "I don't know how I got hooked to Lena," he sighed in despair, sounded remorseful.

It is too late Krish. Instead, think of changing her I suggested.

"She is misguided by her mother," was his only complaint.

"Why couldn't she learn to live with differences in opinions and adjust accordingly" Krish and me tried to reason it out with her but she would not relent.

It is not that Lena is bad but her temperament is offensive. I assured Krish that Lena in her quieter moments feel remorseful. In fact, Krish told me that she attempted rapprochement.

Lena argued, "Just because we are married, should we ignore our individualities? Should there be an agreement at all times and on all occasions?

Krish appeared tolerant, quietly replied, "Is it easy for me to accept everything you say? Alternatively, if you try to convince me about your point of view, would that amount to domination?

"After all, we may differ in our views and perceptions, does that mean we are irreconcilable. Be reasonable," Krish tried to coax her.

She would not change her mind. She countered by arguing "For example recently you accused me of several things, but one which is unfair haunts me."

"Why do you consider that I am out of control? Is it not an insinuation - I raised an issue which is affecting many women. I firmly believe that the archaic belief systems of our women degrade their self-esteem, underestimate their role in their family circles."

"But haven't they disagreed with you, haven't they? Krish quipped. Lena got irritated. "Yes but they latch on to their shackles! They know not what freedom means. I am afraid; they are ignorant of their rights. I want women to be free from fetters - then only they will become more expressive, more honest and certainly more productive- not just settle for making babies and do other menial jobs."

"And, your mom says every family needs a head to lead" she questioned the wisdom of Krish's mother.

"Isn't she right? Every organization however small must have someone to command and demand accountability. What is wrong with it Lena, if I may ask?

"No Krish, this is not an office - in a family all are equal, I do not like to be commanded" she did not mix words.

"In my studies in IIM I have read about many management structures at micro and macro levels. Family organization is no different from business organization."

"Business organizations need profit, promotion and controls. In a family, all are equal. A wife need not toil with a baby, cook the food, and serve while the men give orders; It is nothing but sheer exploitation and nothing else" Lena appeared indifferent and reticent.

Krish smiled "What about love, respect and concern for …." Lena interrupted him, "They are flowery words for servility and serfdom, Krish." "They are invisible tools of exploitation to perpetuate submission and subservience."

"If an element of sacrifice is inconvenient, human relationships become features of hypocrisy. Is not Life a 'give and take adjustment'? In fact, minus sentimentality life becomes business; is there no aesthetic dimension to human bondages."

"It is all a play of words and sentiments. No real substance" Lena brushed aside Krish.

He shuddered to think what awaits him in future. "Parents expect us to behave as per their norms. We do not need to comply with their wishes" Lena brusquely negated husband's suggestion. Krish realized his arguments with Lena counterproductive.

I listened very carefully but urged Krish, "Do not consider this is the end of the world. Leave room for negotiation." "As your mom suggested try to patch up in a calmer and quieter ambience. Go to Boston, start a new life."

I requested Lena to join Krish in Boston before considering the D word. "Change of ambience might help."

After considerable wrangling, she agreed to accompany him to Boston.

"Boston posting might come in handy," his parents Parvathi and Maheswar supported the move.

"You could get a baby made in Boston, US," they joked. Lena did not spare even a second. She instantly replied, "We are not going there to make babies, Aunty." It caused a ripple of unease in Parvati. Nevertheless, Parvathi did not let Lena have the last word "But, elders must always bless for *siri* (wealth), *sampada* (righteous acquisitions) and *satsantanam* (distinct progeny)." Lena laughed away saying "Thank you."

"I want you to wear this diamond necklace. You appear too simple" Parvathi offered one more gesture of traditional honor. "No thanks aunty. I don't like jewelry or cosmetics" Lena declined politely. Parvathi wanted to tell her: Giving haldi, (symbolic of permanent prosperity) *kumkum* (symbolic of happy marital life) along with precious ornaments and silk *saree* is our tradition and are considered auspicious acts. However, Lena appeared indifferent, preferred silence; Parvathi concluded that Lena hates everything connected to tradition.

Parvathi told her husband "She advises people to have a break with the past. Her contention was that they are the traditional tools, with which the elders manipulate young mind to perpetuate subservience to hierarchical family system."

"Times have changed – is it not? People have changed, "Culture gap is widening my dear," Mahesh commented.

Parvathi remembered the hearty welcome Maheshwar's parents arranged.

"My daughter-in-law is *Maayinti Mahalakshmi*.(the goddess of wealth of our house)," Parvathi remembered the affectionate words of her mother-in-law for the new bride. "To show her confidence and faith in me she garlanded me with so many gold ornaments which belonged to the family for generations."

"What a difference" she wondered within herself. "I had to accept them with humility and humbleness. I showed eagerness in taking the gift and expressed gratitude for her act of generosity. When I touched her feet in reverence she hugged me with great affection, blessed me saying 'you have to acquire more wealth, earn name and fame and preserve family prestige."

"Growing culture-gap", Maheswar repeated quietly. He looked at his son "This jewelry belong to Lena whenever she wants," Maheshwar placed the jewel box in his hands.

"She won't like to look gaudy" Krish summed up his wife's liking.

"She might like them later, take these jewels with you." Lena refused to accept them.

"What else can I give her then? Parvathi wondered.

He shrugged his shoulders and casually remarked "Not necessary mom," Parvathi felt snubbed.

"Who bothers? She took the modern looking diamond necklace into her hands; felt insulted, 'Spent 2 lakh rupees; Waste of money' she stuffed the jewel into her handbag.

Maheswar looked at his self-pitying, distraught wife and said "In a lady's lap a happy man must ignore nappy-time mom; don't dig into the past" Maheswar advised his wife not to sulk. He saw his son pretending to keep himself busy settling his wife's belongings.

Empty of words but full of unspoken sentiments father and son looked at each other.

Maheswar broke the silence and said, "There is nothing more to talk." "We leave you both, *bon voyage*" Krish's parents bade farewell. "If you find time ring us once-a-while" Parvathi shook hands with Lena while she was talking to her friends. Krish kept himself busy with packing measures.

Krish recollected his teacher's remark, 'The city of New England is the seat of 'Beer Bellied Board Room Bandits', 'self-seeking tradesmen and self-righteous white people'. But, it is a seat for many institutions of academic excellence. In fact, Maheswar's father studied in the University there.

However, Lena kept wondering what is in store for her in the future; she expressed anxiety about her ailing father.

"You must pass the Immigration Counter. Please proceed," the staff showed the way..

At the immigration counter there were many illiterate laborers going to Middle Eastern countries. The staffs were questioning the validity of their papers. Background bargains are in progress.

"Go ahead sir; you are going to US is it not? Join that Q" the officer directed them to the next counter.

Krish observed the level of bargaining between groups of passengers with the Immigration Officers at the other counter; it was leading to nowhere. He got himself involved in the 'bargain'. "Why not allow them; he gently questioned the officer. "What more proof you need to allow them. They are illiterate and innocent" Krish supported the labor migrants to Middle East.

"You think so. You are wrong. How do you think they came up to this point? They pretend illiterate; could you imagine an innocent laborer from an interior village has that much money or wherewithal to get a passport, buy flight tickets and knowledge to fill various papers? Special 'agents' pick up these people. These people could well be part of human trafficking. They are devils once they are on their own. They may well be drug peddlers. They transport contraband goods and forbidden luggage."

"We know what they are up to. Please, allow us to do our jobs please" the officer sounded pleading. "In fact, some of them if caught by the host countries for over-staying are prepared to be deported. "At the cost of Indian government of course" he emphasized.

"In fact it is worse than Hispanic migration of USA. The Supervising Officer began explaining. Krish was curious to know more but he had to leave them.

"We have very little time to catch our flight," Lena shouted at her husband. They rushed through to the Customs Counter. "Do you have any valuables to declare? Like gold, antiques etc,." Krish nodded his head and said "no"; but the official asked their hand luggage opened.

"You have so many silver items? Have you obtained permission from Reserve Bank of India," Customs official gently enquired.

"No; we never thought of it, it is our personal possession. We are not taking out to sell them. They are being used."

"I agree with you sir. But have you declared that you are carrying them with you?

"No. I have not," Krish admitted. But Lena fired at them, "Why are you harassing us? It is our property and we will take it where we like. Who are you to stop us?

"No. We are not here to harass you but we are here to do our duty. As per law you are required to declare your valuables if they exceed certain limits" he politely answered her.

"I don't think we exceeded our limits" Lena's reply was rash. "Take these people to the other counter and explain" the senior officer ordered his staff.

The junior staff explained what to be done. He gave them a paper and asked them to "Fill the form and declare you will bring back all the valuables which exceeded your limits," the officer appeared very surprised. He called Krish to a side and murmured in low tone.

"Never argue with Customs officials; if they wish they could implicate you as drug peddler. All we are asking you to do is to fill the declaration form." Lena appeared unwilling but Krish had asked her to calm down. He began itemizing the silverware and finally declared that they would be brought back to India. The senior officer looked at the paper; counter signed it below, entered the reference in his passport and allowed them to proceed to the Boarding gate. On their way to the Boarding gate Lena used many four-letter words and accused them to her heart's contentment.

"Those bastards expect some bribe from us. I am glad we did not pay" Lena's anger continued even after they sat in their seats. Krish preferred to keep listening and nodding his head.

The person sitting next to Lena picked up the topic "But madam they claim it is their duty to protect our nation's wealth," he laughed loudly. Completely ignoring the presence of other passengers, he talked like a commander. He looked at Lena with a smile but Krish smiled back suggesting his willingness to talk.

"I am Visu from Madras. I work in Boston as a Consultant to a finance company" he stretched his hands for a handshake.

"I am also in the same business" Krish shook his hands, "It is my first assignment in Boston." Krish casually asked if he knew of his client in Boston; Visu tried to locate Krish's office "Maybe it is located in downtown" a vague reply but confidently said.

"Never mind; Boston is an easy city, it is easy to locate any office. Boston is a highly developed city. Public transport is really the best in the world (that is America of course)." However, Visu's platitudes have intent; the conversation was to dig into Krish's personal life. But,"Thank you" was Krish's brief reply.

After a short lull, Visu tried to prolong the conversation. "If you are a Brahmin it will be easier to understand 'Boston Brahmins', they claim to be puritans, you know" he laughed again. "Nevertheless they are really productive people" he appeared earnest. Astute looking Visu's athletic features, austere get-up and confident talk are impressive. He appears very special and Krish could not but listen to him although he appears tired.

"I am not a Brahmin but he is" Lena suddenly interjected. Krish had to introduce himself. "I am Krishnamachary, Krish for short" he felt Visu's handshake was painful. "My wife Lena Ramlu; we are from Hyderabad" Krish reluctantly revealed his identity.

"I am Viswanathan Nambiar originally from Trivandrum. I am in Boston for the last ten years."

"Before getting to Boston I dreamt about studying in MIST; it never materialized though" he sighed. "If I may ask, where did you work before coming to Boston? Visu inquisitively asked.

"I am with Accenture but assigned to implement a project for a client here in USA," Krish had to give a clue.

"An important assignment I guess" Visu enthusiastically looked at Krish for an answer. Krish was in no mood to reveal anything. He smiled but kept Visu guessing. "Let me know if I could be of help" Visu applied another trick; tried to please his acquaintance.

"Thank you, but our client will be sending a person to Logan Airport. Besides, I know only a little about Boston as I was living in NY during my studies in New York. A former colleague of mine studied in MIST."

Visu took that toehold. He started talking about himself "You know I entered USA on a tourist visa and extended my stay illegally," he proudly admitted. "As I ran out of money, I had no option but to join a restaurant for work. Police arrested me, as I was an innocent but illegal immigrant.

"In the jail, I met a co-prisoner Vinayagar (Vinny), a Tamil Sri Lankan. He admitted he was an over-greedy stockbroker. Surprisingly, he got the cozy refugee status within a few weeks and released from prison. But I later understood he is an Economic-Criminal in Sri Lanka. Actually, he was considered a fugitive as he cheated many of his customers; left Colombo and landed in USA with lots of money." Krish got curious about the story of Visu.

"After a few weeks of Vinny's (Vinayagar) release, I was also released on parole; they pardoned me and eventually granted citizenship. Vinny got a decent job in Boston because of his connections with wealthy white American friends. I understood from his talk, he settled well in Boston with the help of a wealthy Stockbroker."

Having gotten the interest of Krish he continued with more vigor. "It was an accident; may be destiny; I don't know. One day he came to MIST to admit his son in the Engineering faculty; just then I was hanging around MIST to meet a friend. To my surprise, it was Vinayagar (Vinny), clean-shaven, round faced well-built man in a three-piece suit; got down from his Mercedes car and stood in front of me.

"Hai Visu" he greeted me first. I was startled. He embraced me joyously before I could gather myself. His embrace seeped in great affection and excitement; we sat for coffee and conversation in the canteen. During the conversation, he casually asked me if I am looking for a job knowing my computer skills. I readily admitted that I am looking for a job. That was it – he gave me a job. I was to work as his confidant in managing his stock broking activity. My job is to check out the market share of his investments. His job is to pick the best performing shares making the market movement."

Visu sat upright in his seat and seriously said, "I tell you he is a wizard in the finance industry." "You know something; he made his first million soon after I joined him. As a mark of gratitude, he made me his business partner. For me from then on, there is no looking back." Visu's face glowed with pride.

Krish showed earnest interest and appreciation and said "You both must have worked hard - stockmarkets are like gambling houses, one must become a dare devil " he winked with a smile.

Not knowing who Krish really is Visu suggested in a patronising mode "You must meet my partner Vinayagar; I will arrange that meet once you are settled in Boston" he volunteered without Krish's request.

"He has Mida's touch, anything he holds becomes gold."

Krish wondered why he was boasting about Vinny, but kept listening. As Visu continued non-stop, he thought he would try diverting his attention.

"What about your family; have you any children?

Before Krish completed his question he quickly replied "I have a large family, more than 300 active buyers and sellers of shares; in one word I am not married, I devoted my entire life to my job" Visu looked at Krish confidently.

"I am sorry if I offended you in any way" Krish tried to get a break as he was getting sleepy and tired. Visu was mercurial in his response. "No, I am not offended; not at all" Visu laughed away.

"I am not selfish but I am obsessive in my job. Wife, children, dogs, TV's are not my cup of tea." His explosive loud laugh irritated Krish, woke up his wife.

"What happened? Lena woke up, opened her wide eyes, sat upright in her seat.

"Sorry madam, it must the sound of my loud laugh that disturbed your sleep" Visu's impish smile bothered Lena.

"I wondered what caused such an explosive sound." Lena looked at him naughtily.

Visu increased his decibels. "Your husband asked me if I have children." He once again exploded with his boisterous laugh. Lena looked upset, "What is so amusing? She showed her irritation.

"I am not married, that is why" Visu joked. One cannot but notice his garrulous, abrasive and easygoing mannerisms.

"Marriage is a boon for a few but bane for many," he sounded poetic and philosophical.

"Really! She looked amazed. "It is because of women I suppose" she expected language of intolerance and male chauvinism.

"No, in our case, men are the cause for trouble. For example my father was afraid of losing my mother, always jealous of her beauty; but, my mom wanted to be free from all attachments. Unfortunately, my dad's love was my mom's curse," Visu bewailed.

Suddenly Lena felt she lost her pedestal, lost a chance for condemning men for women's oppression.

"Loved or hated 'woman is a woman', weak, submissive or aggressive" Visu simplified his supposition.

"It is unusual, it is almost always the other way round - Are not women the victims of man's impropriety" Lena parried a question. Visu avoided replying.

Lena pointedly asked him "Why not get married? She looked at him weirdly.

"If marriage is an answer I would have been the first one to take it. But it is not….."

Lena interrupted him and said, "I mean it is an alternative to fill the void."

"You may be right" Visu mellowed down looked at his watch avoiding an answer. Lena felt hungry did not continue.

Flight staff announced lunch. Lena did not continue.

'Wake up Krish, it is meal time" Lena woke him up. The airhostesses started arranging table-settings to serve their business class passengers.

"I have ordered fried-chicken for you from the menu," she told Krish. "Good" replied Krish.

"Isn't he a Brahmin" Visu thought of asking but kept quiet.

"He eats every living thing that moves; except us" Lena chuckled casually.

"I noticed Brahmins have a good taste for meat. For example my good friend Iyengar, immensely liked the lamb curry I make. He visits me frequently for the special treat'. Visu noticed Krish's obvious dislike of the conversation, changed the topic.

"I tell you, Air India's selection of wines is so good. Have you ever tasted *Pinonoir* Krish, it goes well with chicken. Have some more," Visu pressed the calling bell.

"Please fill our glasses again" he requested the attending staff. Staff appeared reluctant but served some more wine. "Take it easy sir" warned the staff. Krish and Lena thoroughly enjoyed the wine and started giggling for every joke Visu made.

"You are not married but are you celibate? Lena's blunt question made Visu laugh loudly.

"Show me one who is celibate. Virginity is no more a precondition for love and marriage"

"You are right but I married Krish because I need a husband to work for me" Lena lost control of her speech. "Shut up Lena" Krish got irritated.

"I need no one's permission" Lena appeared drunk and careless.

"I know men; most of them are impotent" she mumbled in tiresome voice. Visu appeared quite stable and kept watching her. Krish stretched himself dosing off in his seat.

"For naughty wives husbands are always impotent," Visu mumbled; laughed at his own comment. "Thank God I am unmarried" he admired himself. Nevertheless, Lena's demeanor provoked Visu. He looked at Lena's bulging boobs and her well built body. "She is certainly not a holy cow" he mulled the thought of befriending her. His mind started troubling him. "Let me try my luck in Boston and get closer to her" he resolved.

Flight arrived at Logan Airport on time.

"Welcome Krishnamachary" Lena spotted a placard holding man in uniform at Logan Airport.

"I am your chauffuer, my name is Richard" he showed another man standing by his side. "He is Mr Kohl, PRO of Mistry and Son Textiles." Visu quickly grasped the importance of Krish.

"Welcome to Boston Sir, Madam." They both welcomed them with a big smile. Visu commanded Richard to load the luggage in the limousine meant for Krish and Lena. PRO Kohl gave his visiting card to Visu.

"I know you make excellent textile products and supply them world wide" Visu complimented Kohl.

Visu once again repeated his offer to Krish. "I realized you are a VIP guest, but you are most welcome to come and stay with me. Although I am single I have a five bed house."

He pulled his visiting card and gave it to Krish "Call me at anytime, I am on the other end of the telephone."

"After settling down we will call you" reciprocated Krish. Visu closed the car door after kissing Lena's hand and bade goodbye to them. However, he conveyed his piercing looks at Lena throwing valentine signals.

PRO Kohl told the limousine's chauffeur, "Let us take our guests to Marriot Hotel."

"It is an hour's drive from here, sir, please relax in the car," Richard the chauffeur advised them. Krish stretched himself almost instantly and said "I had too much to drink on the flight, I have a kind of hangover" Krish explained the cause for his unease. Lena felt equally bad and hence nodded her head indicating it is the case with her too.

"Last summer we were here in the east coast. It was pleasant; but this year summer is quite severe it looks" she commented casually. "Besides the flight was rough" Krish added. His comments evoked no response from Lena. They both snoozed for most of the journey.

"We made special arrangements for you to stay in Marriot sir, if you prefer" Kohl proposed. Lena hinted "I prefer hotel, we will stay there for a few weeks."

Hotel Manager himself came out of his office room to greet them. He bent his head most humbly and greeted them in an oriental way.

"We have bridal suite reserved for you sir, if you follow me" Krish looked at him and asked, "Are you sure? We are married a few weeks back, you know." The manager signaled his awareness by bending respectfully but firmly and asked Krish to follow him.

Krish looked at the bridal suite 'Welcome to Marriot Mr and Mrs Krishnamachary' printed on a red ribbon stretched on the bed. "Unbelievable" he thought.

"You are still newlyweds aren't you? Manager chuckled exposing his golden teeth. "Yes we are married recently" Krish nodded. He looked around; every luxury one can think has existed there without any limitation, "No need to ask us. They are all meant for your use; the choice is yours sir" the manager proudly presented the keys to the room. Luggage arrived within a few minutes.

Hotel Manager looked at Lena while she was unpacking "Spare a few minutes for us in the evening Madame. We wish to follow an old tradition of welcoming newlyweds; if you do not mind."

"That is very sweet of you" Krish shyly accepted his proposal. "Our management holds you in high esteem and instructed me to treat you special" the manager of Thai origin remarked with a gentle smile.

"As you wish" Krish closed the doors after him. Lena overheard their conversation "Why not enjoy their hospitality" she appeared overly indulgent. Jetlag combined with dull and morose outside weather discouraged them to get up from their bed early; slept away until the evening.

However, Krish managed to get up and noticed the time difference between India and US, corrected his watch. All the food on the table and the champagne bottle reminded him that they have not eaten any food since 20 hours. He felt hungry tried to wake up Lena.

"I have to meet the Board of Directors tomorrow at 10.00 in the morning" Krish said it in complaining mood. "What would you like to do, darling" Krish tried petting her, but found Lena uncaring; he sat beside her on the bed but she turned the other side.

"Have something to eat" Krish tried to appease her. "Yes I ate some food in the middle of the night, I am not hungry anymore." "I feel like sleeping" she mumbled; removed his fondling hand placed on her bum. Disheartened Krish went into the bathroom and had a cold shower to cool himself. He felt bored, decided to go to the lobby; found Visu's visiting card in the pocket of his shirt.

Krish rang up Visu almost immediately; "Care to join me for a drink," he sounded a command.

"Sure Krish, give me a few minutes. I will be on my way soon and I know the location of your hotel" Visu rang a little later and said, "I have a Blue Label Whisky, should I bring?

"Oh, no the bar has everything I hope. We will have couple of drinks."

"Would Lena be joining us?

"I guess so, but right now, she feels tired, reluctant even to get up. In any case, we have to get ready for the welcome ceremony by the hotel in the evening hours.

Visu wanted to know why drinks now?

"Just to pass time"

"I could come but..." he was hesitant; but asked "Could I ask you am I allowed to join your private ceremony"

"Not that private any way" he tried some fill words.

Lena appeared tired and disinterested. Krish tried to provoke her by saying they are gathering to convey their best wishes it is just a mark of respect, and also to convey their best wishes for our harmonious and blissful married life" Krish added a note of sarcasm.

"I don't like that mockery Krish; you remember we already had one in Hyderabad" she showed her lack of interest.

"Let us witness one more act, it may be interesting" Krish put a stuffy face but managed a smile. "By the way Visu is joining us."

"Is he? Lena got up from bed reluctantly. "Did you invite him or he invited himself? Lena sounded sarcastic. "You could have told me earlier," Lena complained.

Manager of the hotel came in a hurry searching for Krish and Lena. "As soon as you are ready sir" he bent his head forward in a submissive posture. They both followed the manager to the banquet room.

"You look stunningly beautiful" Visu made a remark usually meant for family members and not expected from a stranger. Krish looked at Visu censoriously. Visu did not bother to take notice of Krish's disdain. He got up from his chair and offered her the seat.

"They are wishing us a very happy harmonious married life" Lena said it jokingly. "They even gave us a bridal suite" Lena put a stuffy face and added a note of artificiality.

"But how did they know" Visu wondered.

"May be my boss, the President of my company in Mumbai; he was the only one I invited for my wedding. Unfortunately, he could not attend the wedding, because of his wife's sudden illness. But he appreciated the fact I was the youngest Vice-President getting married. Since he could not attend, as compensation, he promised us honeymoon in USA. I never knew he meant it seriously. He may have assigned me this prestigious assignment for that reason," Krish looked bemused.

Visu looked at Lena and said, "Isn't that wonderful" he admired the extravaganza of the ambience. "Thank you" Lena acknowledged his comments, shook her head gaily.

Visu requested Krish to accept the toast of honor by him. "Sure Visu. You are welcome," he hugged him cozily. "I am unaware and unprepared to do this but I consider this an honor" Visu also felt he is inadequately dressed for the occasion.

Next day the Hotel made excellent arrangements and assembled a few to witness the function. Visu raised his glass of champagne and wished "Happy days to you both." "This big 'He-man' is lucky to have such a beautiful bride. He deserves our heartiest congratulations and best wishes for a happy married life," Visu's toast followed claps from the small audience.

"It is for you both from your boss, in Mumbai, it arrived yesterday," Manager handed a beautiful package. His staff brought a big flower bouquet and gave a greeting card. Visu volunteered to read it. It said, "You guys got two years in Baltimore, enough to return as wholesome three," Visu handed it to Lena. She received it with a grin on her face.

"Real surprise for you madam, this Pashmina shawl is especially for you – it is the best of its kind." Visu opened the pack; placed it on her shoulders. "You deserve many more gifts; the first and best gift your parents gave you is this man called Krish. Enjoy him." He looked at Krish with a mischievous smirk.

"Champagne is heady enough," Krish said while drawing Lena close to his chest. "You are great my dear" he giggled embracing her with a kiss. Lena pulled herself away chiding him.

"Bacon is really great, eat it; Visu served two more slices." These bacon slices are from young pork belly; they are as tasty as Kerala's young coconut's kernel" Visu relished the food. "Blue label whisky with it" he ordered the server. Hotel staff left the room leaving Krish, Lena and Visu for their privacy.

"A great dinner" Krish could hardly speak coherently. Lena appeared drunk; she waited to finish the final round of her drink; expected Krish to take her to the room.

A few minutes passed. "I can't even lift myself, I am sleepy," she said with a garbled speech. Krish equally inebriated requested Visu, "Take her to the room Visu," he threw his hand in the air signaling his slapdash attitude. Lena mumbled some abuse, rashly pulled herself from the chair but fell into the embrace of Visu.

Visu hesitated to go further. "Don't be nervous - you fool, yesterday you were a bloody limping bastard, she waved her hand pointing at his pants.

"I am sure it is the Champagne that kicked you in the right place, at last you got the effect of Viagra"" she giggled; she drew him closer and embraced him tightly.

Visu got up quickly, zipped his pant and rushed out leaving drowsy Lena, naked on the bed. "I want you again," she shouted but Visu rushed back to Krish leaving drowsy Lena.

Krish appeared very drunk and sleepy, placed his head on his hands kept crossed on the table, not aware of what was happening around. Visu thought of asking hotel staff's help but did not. He took care and managed to take him to the room; kept Krish on the bed beside Lena.

Next morning Krish woke up lazily to find Lena naked; shoes on one side and clothes dispersed everywhere.

"I want you again," muttered Lena in her dreamy state. Krish got up in spite of his hangover, had no energy to gather her things.

"Last night how could you manage so well," Lena blabbered in her dream state. After sometime, she woke up, got a doubt whether it was real or dream after all; but felt shy, and covered her naked body with a blanket.

"Last night you thrilled me" she wanted to thank her husband. Krish remained dull, did not respond to her sex talk; but managed to repeat his admiration, "Last night you looked stunningly beautiful." He did not care to ask why she was asking such searching questions.

"You are very cold now," she smiled with an expectation of cuddling or kissing.

"I can't remember last night," he replied sleepily. Lena shocked but remained silent, sat up on the bed and wondered about the events of the night.

"But who brought me here? She looked around; her shoes, skirt, shirt, and underwear everything was laying helter-skelter on the floor.

"Who undressed me? She tried to gather her memory.

"I don't remember; Visu may have brought you here." Krish sounded casual and turned himself away from her. "What happened to you then" she pretended anger. "I was dead drunk, too much champagne and whisky, I am sure."

"It must be Visu," half-sleepy Lena pondered. She could not ignore the pleasantness of the experience, but felt cheated. She silently gathered her dress but kept thinking. Krish fell off to sleep again sounded snoring.

"It must be that fellow," she confirmed but thought of Visu as dirty and dishonest.

She was deeply disappointed that Krish did not make love to her in the night. She resented the fact that Krish allowed some stranger to intrude; cursed him as useless, impotent, clueless and shameless.

"If you can't satisfy a woman's sexual desire, what good it is to claim Vice-presidency of this or that multinational? She reflected on Krish. Although, Lena never was averse to having multiple sex partners before marriage; but after marriage she did not like to cheat, she told herself.

She felt like cleaning herself; looked at her image in the mirror, felt guilty. "Krish let me down in many ways." Her anger grew, felt like slapping him, but found him flat on the bed snoring.

"I was raped you shameless fool" she despised to see her image in the mirror.

She felt haunted by the words of a wise man. "Sex is an important carnal function; but it should not induce immorality; it should not make you mean, slavish, selfish, and jealous." "Body pleasures grant us an iota of pleasure but can add a donkey load of burden."

The Wiseman urged his followers, "Make your mind an unending reservoir of creativity, consciousness. Do not lose it for the sake of body pleasures."

"But how? She mulled.

Why wise men make us guilty?

She was visibly disgusted, pulled her hair in anger, got up with intense headache.

Suddenly fear engulfed her. "What if Krish knows it." "Not a chance" she assured herself. Another thought came to her mind, "Why should I fear, he himself may have encouraged

Visu; after all Krish knows he is sexually ineffective even with *Viagra*."

Lena openly challenged him, gave him few months time to get better. She forewarned Krish if psychotherapy and medicines proved ineffective, she would divorce him any way. Besieged by many negative thoughts, she became awake and restless.

"He knows that I fight for women's rights which include everything; includes sensitive issues such as right to have satisfying sex. If the partner is ineffective she must enjoy the right to sleep with whom she likes, just as men." "In any case he knows that I am not a virgin and that he is not the first man I had an affair before."

She argued for both sides in the 'court' of her own mind. "What about loyalty to one another? Her inner voice questioned.

"Loyalty is not servility, loyalty is binding to the truth, face the truth, not the façade."

"What is the truth here?

"The truth is his failure to meet the expectation of marriage and love." "Failing on promises, expectations made to each other, out of wedlock relationships etc. is a serious crime. Is it not the duty of Krish to satisfy me in bed? "Am I asking too much? She continued fighting with herself.

"Have some patience, marriage is 'once a life-time' affair. After all he is also looking for happiness."

"But now, I am within my right to do what I like for myself. I am entitled to my happiness."

The duel between the two halves of Lena's inner self went on for a while but her final option was self-seeking and defiance.

Krish appeared quite unaware of last night's incidence.

Anyhow, while in Boston Krish was kept busy, as he had to lead the negotiating team to sort out differences between the agents of Mistry and agents of Kenn and Dunn. His busy schedules involved frequent travels between Boston, NY, Texas and India. Therefore, Krish and Lena decided to continue their stay in Marriot for a few more weeks.

"By the way Lena, I may have to go to New York for two days. Would you like to join me; you could meet your old pals," Krish looked at her suggestively.

"No Krish, I rather stay here" she did not elaborate but sounded un-interested. "I wonder if you could call Visu to help me out if at all I wanted to go out for shopping or other entertainment."

Krish gave an abrupt answer, "No I have not." "He might be busy with his own business," Lena sounded nonchalant.

"Call Visu and ask him if he could help me in shopping if I feel like going out" she gently requested him again.

Krish appeared reluctant "Sure, but why not go on your own. Our hotel will take you on a limousine."

Lena looked lovingly at him, added in a soft tone "No, I am not that keen; first of all I must ring my dad in Hyderabad and a few friends in New York. Let me therefore stay back," Lena blabbered some fill-words.

Krish obliged his wife and called Visu almost immediately; phone rang but no answer; Krish left a clear message "Call Lena, she might need your help."

"I left a message; he may answer you later. But I got to go to meet Mistry Bhai; he called me several times," Krish hurried himself with a briefcase.

In fact Mistry Bhai Textiles started negotiating with US based Kenn and Dunn International, the world famous suppliers of readymade suits, shirts, dresses, uniforms etc. Accenture has sent Krish to manage a deal for Mistry after careful evaluation of the Kenn and Dunn Company's profile.

Visu tried to ring up Krish without success. Although he found that there were more than half a dozen calls from Lena. He feared a ton of bricks on his head from her; he justified his trepidation.

"She must be ringing to scold me, threaten me" he mulled the possibility of rough talk. He wondered if she ever recognized his making love that night in the hotel while she was drunk. Visu considered confessing, asking her to forgive him.

He told himself many times, "It is not me but she invited me" he tried to ease himself from guilt feeling. He pitied her also. "I don't blame her either; I heard from her own mouth that Krish is incapable of satisfying her in the bed. Moreover how could I resist the beauty of such a voluptuous fairy?" "After all, she induced me into the act. I don't think I should blame myself," Visu has become increasingly introspective.

"Hereafter, you should not go near her," he scolded himself. "If she were a spinster I would have no hesitation, but a married woman…" he banged his head with his hand. "But the pleasure she gave was mind boggling; gave me heaven on earth" that very thought made him excited. His senses craved for her company. Krish's voice in his message on the answering machine also sounded very friendly.

Lena rang him again. This time her voice mail sounded different. "I need your help Visu; Krish had gone to NY for three days," he felt greatly relieved of the burden of guilt.

He was surprised, "After all Lena is not complaining. Thank God, she was not aware of my involvement" he once again assured himself, answered the call.

"I am sorry Lena I forgot my personal mobile at home; I could not get your message until I returned from my business trip" he managed to cover up.

"Tell me what I can do for you" he was spirited in his words. "I am alone, Krish is gone for a few days; would you care to come to me" Lena sounded pleading. "I will be happy if you could come," she urged. Visu got the message and he recollected his last time visuals of Lena.

"I must see her" he could not get over the compelling desire. His morals took a backseat.

Emboldened by Lena's open invitation he set aside all his inhibitions, justified his decision to go to Lena. "She desires me; she certainly enjoyed my company."

Got himself dressed as a young man; wore a t-shirt, which read, "I intend to park where I am allowed" unlike the words printed on the bikini of his ex-girlfriend, which read 'don't park here without permission'.

"I have Rothschild's vintage wine. Would you fancy," he asked her over the phone. "Bring, if it is good and If available some chicken from the Indian restaurant." Lena's sexy voice sounded music to him. "I will be with you in a few minutes Lena," he conveyed that he is ready for an affair.

For a moment, he felt sad and guilty, "Poor Krish; he is a good looking guy but lacks virility. It is a pity Lena's enticing figure could not raise his sex passion."

"Yes. She has every reason to seek her avenues to happiness," he reasoned his flirt with another man's wife.

"I know you are that rascal making love to me that night. But you are a good rapist. I registered every move of yours" she smiled mischievously, and flattered him with many more kisses.

"Listen Visu; Krish is away for few days again. I want you again," she insisted. Visu spent that night in her arms and embrace.

Thus, Lena got used to the idea of Visu satisfying her every so often. Unsurprisingly, their relationship became a talking point for the staff of the hotel.

Visu read the morning paper Boston Globe which carried news item "Indian man murdered his wife and her lover, scattered the body parts in different areas of East Coast, New York and Washington," Visu suddenly became jittery after reading.

He walked out of Lena's room, took the lift, and entered the lobby; suddenly found Krish talking to someone in the lobby area.

Taken aback Visu did not know what to say. He questioned, "Haven't you gone to NY? Visu's voice muffled as he saw Krish. He felt jilted, spontaneously zipped his jumper, concealing a suggestive message on his t-shirt 'I wish to park here with permission'." Krish appeared unconcerned.

"Yes I went there but I just returned, to surprise Lena," he smiled. "Our meeting got postponed till next Monday because of sudden illness of the main man," Krish clarified.

"Care to join me for a drink? Krish's innocent invitation confirmed Visu's assumption that he is not a suspect. Nevertheless, he could not recover from the initial shock.

"What if he saw us in the act? He trembled in his pants and sweating in great fear.

He fumbled for words but managed to reply coherently. "You keep going, I can't join you now as I will have to go home" he left him at once pretending hurry.

Visu rushed to his car, sank into the car seat with a sigh of relief, stretched his legs in a prostrated posture, lighted a cigarette and exclaimed loudly "Thank god." Wiped sweat from his forehead, "Thank god I am saved."

"That sex-maniac, hooked me into this mess", he blamed Lena. He slapped his face himself, felt overwhelming fear and guilt. He considered warning Lena "Never ever again" he censured himself.

He pulled himself up jerked forward, sat up, picked up his mobile and shouted into it in a panicky voice "Krish is back. He is talking to someone in the lobby," he warned her. Took a few puffs of fag to recover from shock.

Lena called him back while he was driving home. "Krish hasn't come to the room yet. Are you sure it is Krish," Lena sounded least bothered or panicked.

"Never mind Lena, god saved me really, luckily we got away" his voice quivered. That narrow escape shook Visu out of his wits. "Never again" he cautioned himself.

❖❖❖

Memories started haunting Visu. He wondered how the relationship with Lena reached this level of intimacy. One question to which he found no answer is how to get out of the relationship.

He regretted that things started happening very much to his dislike. He recounted his weaknesses. He could not get over his attraction to Lena; fully sympathized with Lena and her predicament.

He recollected Lena's repeated complaint. "Do you know he blames me saying I am sex maniac,." "Tell me is it wrong to expect sex satisfaction from one's own husband? Do I have to suffer this punishment" Lena' self-pity and despair clouded his discretion.

"I fell into this trap, one side Lena and the other side my own lust" he regretted the mess he created for himself. He could not overcome his mental agony; overwhelmed by fear and anxiety he started blaming himself.

Lena made it clear she does not want to part with him; but "She made me her sex slave." He blamed everybody including himself.

Visu tried to convey his fear and share his distress with Lena. "I am scared of the repercussions," he conveyed his worry. "I may have to stop seeing you," he told her.

"In that case I will commit suicide," she blurted instantly. "I thought you are the only one that understood me. If you abandon me I have nowhere else to go." "You are the only one that made me happy" her praise overwhelmed Visu.

After so much introspection, he mustered his self-confidence to ask her an awkward question.

"If you are so much interested why not leave him and come to me?

"Why not divorce him?"

Lena got irritated; she did not reply him immediately. "I wish I could," she muttered in low voice after a few minute's pause and lamented, "I am helpless Visu; my dad threatened me by saying, 'If you make your marriage fail I will kill myself in shame'." Lena broke down in tears while repeating her father's threat. Visu tried consoling her; came back to her when Krish was away.

After recovering from the sadness, she paused again for a while, looked at Visu vaguely with tear-filled eyes "Dad is sick because of massive heart attack and brain stroke. I do not want him to die because of me. The least I can do is not to become a cause for his death." Visu placed his fingers on her mouth and stopped her while coaxing her not to cry. He wiped her tears with his fingers, tried to assure that all will be well.

Somehow, Lena regained from self-pity as Visu made moves to stimulate her. Eveready Lena lured him into action. That gave him heavenly feeling.

Visu forgot everything while making love to her; fortunately, Krish was away in New York for more than a week. Lena had neither remorse nor guilt.

'Morals are for weak and freaks' he remembered Lena's earlier comment in a general conversation.

In his euphoria, Visu shared Lena's essential belief that sex is the essence of life.

Visu reminisced the past; started recounting his past efforts to get married; and how his uncle in Kerala tried to help him.

"You are getting over aged for young brides," his uncle goaded him to get married. "I am not choosy uncle – I will marry whomever you suggest. I follow your advice, I promise." Visu virtually begged him.

"Are you sure you are not having any heart throb in USA" his uncle tried sweet-talk and cajoled him to come out with truth. Visu got irritated but swore on the book of Gita, declared, "I never entertained premarital sex so far. God will punish me if I told you a lie." His uncle stopped him.

"Enough; do not swear, it is not necessary. I believe you; but others may not. I know you wish to settle in life with a traditional wife," he stopped Visu. "Let me see" he went into self-probing, a trance like state, scratched his head tried to recollect. Visu took care not to disturb him, watched him with silence.

"Yes I remember now" he got up and said "come with me." He took Visu into his bedroom. He searched a cupboard took out a brown cover and pulled out a photo. He gave the photo to Visu and asked after a few seconds "What do you say."

"A good looking woman" Visu was brief.

"She is a bride," he said loudly. "If you like I can contact them straight away and ask them for a meeting" he dialed a number.

"My nephew is here. If you wish, you could meet him," he briefed him about Visu.

"I saw a good-looking young lady recently completed her M.Tech. I know her parents - they both are teachers. I casually mentioned about you and suggested that if interested you would meet the girl. Her parents showed great interest but with one condition; you should know that the girl desperately wants to go to USA. They are hoping that an American bridegroom could get her visa. I guess you suit their needs" he commented with a sarcastic smile. He added, "I can never understand the recent developments. Now-a-days girls are demanding foreign careers, foreign degrees etc and brides are bargaining for US visa, you know."

Visu found no reason to doubt the legitimacy of their demands. "Nothing wrong with that uncle – they are justified, because they have to live with total stranger. There are any numbers of cheats on both sides."

His uncle then pulled out a photo of the would-be bride and showed it to Visu. He found the girl is pretty having sharp features. He readily consented.

"Our daughter wants to meet the boy" Girl's parents arranged a face-to-face meeting in a hotel. "I am 35 years old Viswanathan from Boston settled in US for the last ten years" Visu introduced himself pompously. He did not hesitate to declare, "I like you but I do not know if age disparity between us discourages you" Visu gently aired his anxiety. 26-year-old Sarita "Your age is not a problem for me. I agree to marry you but you must help me to go to MIST in Boston" she showed him her academic credentials and showed the copy of her application for student visa.

"MIST granted me admission into the electronic engineering faculty, but I must find money for all the expenses – to get Visa and air tickets etc. I do not have money even to pay for visa fees, let alone pay for my semester fees in thousands of dollars." Visu understood her frustration. He sensed her anxiety and her readiness to marry him.

"Look Sarita you do not need marry me to get to USA. I can loan it to you. You richly deserve all my support" he made an unconditional offer.

Sarita quickly corrected herself. I am just suggesting this could benefit both of us."

"It is no problem. I am in USA for more than a decade. I am allowed to take my spouse with me. I will be more than happy to pay for your studies" Visu assured her.

"Before you agree I want you to take your time to think and then decide" he preferred to imbue his American values.

"Could I get two days to think" Sarita asked for time to answer. "My parents have received another proposal. I am not happy with the boy's parents – they are boisterous and dominating us because we are poor." She expressed her resentment quite clearly.

Visu was never a believer of God that grants material goodies because gods got pleased with prayers. "It is foolish to expect god to be your Genie in a bottle," he was arguing with his friends. But, this time he sincerely prayed god to grant him the fortune of marrying Sarita.

"God answered my prayers. Sarita agreed to marry me" he bragged. Visu thanked god for His mercy.

Her parents organized the ritual of engagement. Sarita's father spoke thanking Visu. "God's ways are many. Your uncle casually mentioned about you living alone in Boston. When I got the details I got the chance to mention my daughter's admission in MIST and I wished to send her there after marriage. But now everything worked out well because of Destiny -it can make or mar our future. Our daughter is lucky and I sincerely thank your uncle," observed Sarita's father.

Next day's news shocked the world. Frightening flash news: "Al Qaeda bombed World Trade Center. Thousands were killed." Newspapers commented that America is tightening the rules of entry of immigrants. They are suspecting all colored people.

Sarita's parents were shocked and understood the complexity of Visu's predicament. "All colored people are under scanner," the newspapers wrote. Visu doubted his own future, decided to go back to US immediately.

Since Betrothal ceremony was over on the condition stipulated by bride's parents, Visu gave a few thousand dollars to Sarita toward her travel arrangements to get to US. Since her grades were excellent, he found no problem in getting her to US. In fact, by then Visu and his business partner Vinayagar were flourishing beyond their belief. Money was not a problem.

Visu confidently gave thousand dollars to his fiancé (would be wife's) travel arrangements before leaving India. He told his uncle that Goddess of Wealth (Lakshmi) has blessed him hence he can afford to give that much to Sarita.

"What if they change their mind? His uncle warned. Visu brushed aside his skepticism.

Despite all travel hazels, he reached Boston and gave a big party to his friends.

"She is my lucky charm": he declared with great pride. She will bring luck to me."

He did everything to get her admission into MIST and paid her fees and other expenses. After the din and dust of 9\11 settled, Sarita, his- fiance arrived.

"Marriage is only a formality" Sarita agreed to live with him with a view to get married eventually.

"I know you prefer to get married, but 'Living together' is quite fashionable in India" Sarita mesmerized Visu into silence by her charming sex-appealing gesture. "But we will get married in India soon after my Ph D. My parents are making elaborate plans for our wedding," declared Sarita with a naughty smile.

"You know that I don't want to go back to India without my citizenship papers in hand" She emphasized her goal clearly.

"It might take years you know" exasperated Visu urged her to rethink. She did not budge but continued living with him at his expense until she completed her studies.

"Now that I submitted my thesis I will go away for a few days to visit my friends" Sarita explained her plans of outing with friends for a few days.

"I know you are very busy Visu," she appeared sad but covered up with a naughty smile.

"If I am free I would have joined you, but never mind, we will have good time soon in India after our marriage." He encouraged her to wear the best dress and jewels; he packed them neatly.

"I am sorry I can't join you right now but enjoy your holidays and come back soon; we must make plans for our travel to India." He hugged Sarita from behind and whispered in her ears "Think about our wedding plans in India." She lustily kissed him several times. A friend of hers took her in her car.

Since then he did not hear about her whereabouts for more than a weak. Strangely, she was not answering her mobile also. Visu panicked, started ringing her contacts. Some of them advised him to wait for a few days more but many said they have no news.

"Two weeks gone but no news about Sarita", Visu told his partner Vinny. "Let me ask my friend' he advised Visu to calm down. "What could have happened? He began inquiring.

Before going to the police, Vinny sought the help of his friend in a MIST affiliated institute. "What is wrong, she got happily married a few days back and is on honeymoon to Hawaii. No time to invite you guys – may be" Vinny's friend appeared cool, oblivious of the reasons of panicking by Vinny and Visu. Visu nearly collapsed hearing the news but manage to walk back to his car. Vinny double-checked the available details. He gathered some more information about Sarita's whereabouts after marriage.

"She is married to her guide Dr.Whiston, a white American man" Vinny hesitated before telling him the details of what transpired. Vinny walked a few steps away to confirm the information but found Visu was pulling out of car park rashly making screeching noise.

"Bitch" Vasu banged his hand on the steering wheel, shouted many four-letter abuses, and drove away in his car leaving Vinny behind. In fact, Vinny had to order a taxi to reach Visu's house.

"She pretended that she is going on holidays, it seems" Vinny was unsure of what exactly was the reason for her abandoning her long-term fiancé. He knew of Visu's dreams of getting married in India.

"To the best of my knowledge they appeared a happy couple. In fact, Vinny told his wife "You and me are supposed to act as Visu's parents" (as per the requisites of Hindu marriage), as Visu lost his parents when he was young" Vinny sadly informed his wife of the unexpected happenings.

Vinny took a taxi and reached Visu's house within a few minutes. Visu appeared hurling away Sarita's clothes, books and her other belongings.

"Did you hear this name Whiston before from Sarita? I gathered some information about her, which I want to check with you." Visu appeared distraught; in his anger, he pretended he has not heard Vinny. Walking through the rubble he tried to caution him, "Take care Visu you may hurt yourself," Vinny tried to pacify him.

"I don't care Vinny." He appeared indifferent for a while and replied brusquely "She must be bitching with him too." In the middle of all the clutter and rubble, he appeared losing his ability to stand. He sat on the ground sobbing, "I gave her utmost of all the best I could afford. She used me, like a doormat," Visu cried like a child.\

Vinny's attempts to console him were futile. He tried to pacify his friend by talking about legal action. "We must lodge a complaint of cheating," he said.

"I have no proof to show that we were living together" writhing pain was visible on his face; he decants his scorn.

Vinny tried to analyze, "Someone must have suggested her 'marriage of convenience' to get the permanent visa. "I guess she must be planning that in absolute secrecy."

Visu kept recounting her recent conversations. "She told me that she will not go to back to India without the American citizenship papers" he continued.

"I sensed her strong wish and even suggested that we should get married here; and we could register our marriage - start the process of 'Naturalization' but her excuse was that she wanted traditional marriage in India. I believed her words as genuine."

"Of late I noticed she was coming late in the nights but I never suspected her"

"She must be planning this since a longtime" Vinny shared Visu's annoyance. "Her goal was to become a citizen of USA. She must be searching means and methods to achieve that," he added.

"You know I tried to help her – I even borrowed money from you to pay for her studies. I never ever suspected her motives," he continued in his sadness.

"I sincerely believed she is my wife until this day" he continued to grieve.

"That ungrateful woman preferred to cheat you. It is simply unbelievable," Vinny totally agreed with him. "Let us see if she left any clues of her intentions." After a thorough search of her study room Vinny found a brief note in her old hand bag. The computer printed note mentioned, "I will be marrying a white American teacher-guide for the sake of naturalization (US Citizenship)….." Vinny read it loudly.

Visu bent his head in apparent sadness and said, "She is treacherous. She could dupe me without giving any hint." "Her pretension is what I cannot comprehend" he went on cursing her and his fate. "My uncle warned me but I was eager to get married."

"Whatever, she is utterly brutal. She is of the kind of person that "Bite the hand that feeds." "She will pay for her sins" Vinny commented.

Visu continued in deep distress and depression. From then on, his disbelief and disillusion became a part of his behavior.

"This is not good" Vinny persuaded him to get back to work, "It might divert your attention" Visu remained silent, enervated and dejected. He could hardly manage to speak a few words.

"Give me a few more days. I will take a little tour of America," Visu appeared indifferent to what he was saying.

"Ok with me - if that is what you think is good for you," Vinny conceded.

However, Visu took time off to track down the whereabouts of Sarita. He did not leave Boston.

Suddenly, Vinny confronted Visu near the Institute. Visu appeared raggedy in tattered clothes, unkempt hair completely worn out.

"Haven't you gone out of Boston" Vinny hugged him affectionately. He felt a hard object touching his chest. Vinny noticed it but waited until he took Visu home.

As soon as he reached home, Vinny suddenly pushed Visu on to the sofa and pulled out the revolver he was hiding.

"What is this Visu? He appeared shocked.

"Are you crazy? Vinny unloaded and took it away from him. "What was the necessity to carry a weapon? He looked at him in annoyance

"Kill someone? He shouted at Visu.

"Yes, I would like to kill Sarita and kill myself" Visu looked like someone possessed. "Yes I bought this gun to kill her"

"Kill Sarita? Does it solve your problem or make you a hero you stupid fellow? He shook Visu violently. Soft-spoken Vinny became furious. "You want to ruin yourself for the sake of that woman? Is that your wisdom? Come on my friend…be sensible. Get back to your senses" he kept on chiding Visu. Visu appeared languid, like a thief caught on site.

"I am twenty years senior to you and I have witnessed many ups and downs in life, life-threatening murderous situations. Violence never resolved any problem. On the other hand it makes it worse." He paused a while "Are you listening to me? Shook Visu one more time and yelled "Control yourself, don't fall into the trap of hatred and revenge." He stopped talking to Visu called his wife to bring the car at once, to Visu's house. Vinny's wife Luckie came in rushing and found blank faced Visu worn to shreds. She wanted to say something but Vinny warned her to keep silent.

He pulled Visu from the sofa as he refused to budge forcibly took him by his collar to his car, forced him into the back seat and sat beside him. "Let's go home," he instructed his panicking wife Luckie.

Vinny and Luckie restrained Visu in their home for ten days. It took more than weekdays for Visu to regain himself, got back to his senses.

"It is a matter of deep hurt because of deceit, insult and shame." "After all the pretensions of love and lust, she literally 'plunged a dagger in his back." Vinny and Luckie sympathized with Visu and guarded him. Slowly Visu recovered from his anger, hatred, and self-destruction.

Before leaving their home Visu expressed his gratitude, "I am fine now. I thank you both, I am sorry I caused you so much worry" Visu touched Vinny's feet in reverence.

"You gave me rebirth" a few tears rolled down his cheek.

"I am more than grateful to both of you. You protected me from endangering myself." He looked at Luckie with tears rolling out "You are more than my mother" Visu touched her feet. She lifted him from the floor, hugged him and cautioned him "Take care, never think of violence. You come from the land of Budha and Gandhi. Be tolerant, be bold" she patted his back as Visu left Vinny's home.

Visu later wrote to his uncle in Kerala narrating the events "My partner Vinny did not allow me to stay alone and, I survived that nasty experience, thanks to Vinny."

From then on Visu became utterly cynical. He became sour, dejected and decided to remain unmarried.

Visu became profoundly philosophical. He approached an elderly man. He told him "Learning from experience is never complete. Exercising caution will be situation-specific and it can never be all-inclusive. Destiny overrides caution and control, ordains the pairs of givers and takers of blame or fame. It selects events, people and perspectives. It prepares the ambience in which the recipient will have little choice."

In Visu's case destiny decided nature of trouble, the proximity of trouble-giver and the necessity of others intervention. The pretext is compassion, protection and preservation of friendship.

Hardly two years passed another incident in which he had to intervene. An unexpected incident occurred. He had to intervene in the affairs of an estranged wife thrown out of her house by the husband. Morally compelled Visu knew her and her family back home before, had to take care of her.

Vinny warned him "You haven't learnt any lesson."

Visu pleaded, "She had no one to care." "I pity her. She is the only daughter of a very popular Catholic School teacher cum priest. Poor girl she is recently married."

Vinny looked cynical. "My feeling is you trust people on their face." "You play by instincts; instincts may work in buying shares or businesses, not persons and emotions. Anyhow try and keep your distance from problems, especially matrimonial problems" Visu thanked his partner but he could not overcome his sympathy for the helpless woman. He gave her shelter, food and financial help in her fight against her husband.

The struggle between the newly married man and wife became bitter; vexed with her husband she wanted divorce. She claimed domestic violence and threat to life as her reasons.

The man claimed that she still maintains illicit extra-marital relationship with her former lover, but agreed to continue marital life if she stops entertaining her former lover. She claimed, "He is planning to kill me."

She convinced Visu that she has enough proof against her estranged husband's psychopathic plans.

She begged, "Help me and save my life," she cried. Her poor relatives from India urged him to help her. Thus forced into the situation he committed that he will fight on her behalf. He spent a lot of money to help her but the woman could not prove the grounds of domestic violence and her perception of death. Husband disputed the facts and refused to give divorce. The woman preferred to go back to India and live with her parents. She had no choice but to leave the country never to return.

Visu entertained the idea of marrying her if she wanted. "She preferred to go back to her ex-lover. I did not mind that. But minimum courtesy demands that she should inform me" he complained to his friends.

"She may have feared you demanding repayment of financial support you gave her," his friends suggested.

"I told her not to worry about repayment. I know she comes from a very poor family. I never expected her to return the money I spent on her."

The unwanted outcome of this affair is that her husband became Visu's enemy number one. "You supported her and destroyed my future," the man bitterly complained. Both incidents transformed Visu completely. "I am a free man. I can choose any woman without any commitment of marriage," declared a garrulous Visu.

Ever since he got involved with Lena he defied his mind and told himself "Life must go on."

"She electrified my sex life. She is bloody good; she gave me new lease of life. Nothing wrong in demanding good sex" he pleaded with his questioning mind. "I know she is married but she is a willing partner. I am not responsible if she is cheating her husband" he hid himself from the reality.

But his mind did not spare him. "It is not that easy mister, if caught in the act Krish may crucify you." His inner self cautioned him. The very thought frightened him, with a chill that ran through the spine.

On the same day, he read a news item: 'A jealous husband murdered his wife and her lover and dispersed the body parts in different places'.

"Lucky Krish did not see me in the act," he thanked stars. He remembered the old saying 'deceit, debauchery, and murder can never be suppressed – they always get revealed, truth can never be altered nor suppressed'. His mind kept damning him. Tired in the act of self-introspection he lost himself and finally resolved not to see Lena any more.

After so much of stormy introspection, he got tired and slept; woke to repeated phone calls.

"I am sorry if I woke you," Vinny sounded apologetic.

"No Vinny, I haven't gone to bed yet."

"I need to meet you in person right now, very urgently" he recognized haste in Vinny's voice. "I will be with you in a few minutes time,."

Before Visu could say, "come down", Vinny hang up the phone. He began worrying if Vinny knew about his affair with Lena.

"He may be coming here to warn me" Visu contemplated that remote possibility. His wandering mind came to a halt Vinny stopped his car in the driveway. Visu rushed out to meet him.

"A great news Visu" Vinny's face glowed with excitement. "I just got some information from our 'agent' Vinay in Delaware."

"You mean the bank fellow," Visu signaled low estimate of the man.

"No we don't need to trust him that much. He told me that a man called Krishnamachary is here in Boston to negotiate with Ken and Dunn on behalf of a Bombay based family firm Mistry and Son. I suddenly remembered you mentioning that name. As we planned earlier, we may get a chance to expand our business. Now the opportunity is knocking our door" Vinny's excitement is obvious.

Visu continued in his melancholy, "Hold on Vinny…. I understand that is a done-deal. They might have reached an agreement by now. Krish is here for the last 6 weeks to finalize the agreement."

"No Visu, they are facing a hitch. Vinay told me the elder Mistry and his son is having divergent opinions."

Vinny affectionately placed his hand on Visu's shoulder and walked a few steps, pleading with him passionately. "Vinay told me Mistry's bid is for 220 million. I know for sure, Ken and Dunn are worth more than half a Billion. They are selling away their company because of internal wrangle; and legal proceedings are looming large, it seems."

"It is impossible Vinny. I know Krish is here to finalize the deal. Don't believe that half-knowledged Vinay," he emphatically declared," "Their negotiations are still in a limbo."

Visu appeared unconvincing. He nodded his head to indicate his disbelief, added, "How could we enter the stage in this late hour? Visu's dismay was obvious.

"I have a plan Visu – you only can make it work" Vinny piercingly looked at Visu and continued, "If only you agree with me."

"It really is in your hands Visu," Vinny appeared beseeching. Although, earnest in his appeal he sounded commandeering.

Suddenly panic overwhelmed Visu.

"We are talking about half billion dollars business," Vinny persuaded.

"Tell me how I can manage to grab the deal as you say? Visu sat beside Vinny; looked at him inquisitively.

"Now you are talking" Vinny smiled. "All you have to do is to befriend Krishnamachary and get an overview of the deal and at what stage it stalled; depending on that information we could work out a strategy to enter into the fray." "If we could offer better bid than Mistry's," Visu stopped him in the middle of his talk.

"As I sensed from Krish he wants to maintain absolute secrecy of his existence here as a negotiator" Visu hesitated. "None of his family or friends knew of his existence here" he tried to cold shoulder Vinny's excitement. "He keeps himself incognito" he added.

He brushed aside Visu's doubts. "That is impossible. If it is such a secret, how could I get to know this? Let us not imagine things like that." He leaned over Visu and in a low voice said, "If necessary, use the bait of money or position." "Use your judgment Visu" "I think you could befriend him, offer a million or two as his fees or CEO job of the new company." "Somehow make him our man" Vinny cheekily smiled with a glint in his eye.

Visu did not respond immediately as he appeared pondering. "I may have to accept that my downfall is inevitable."

"Would I get caught in the muddle of seduction, sex and cheating? Yes, I will be – on one hand I have Lena; she won't leave me; on the other I am addicted to her lovemaking. One day or the other Krish will get to know this …." Visu mulled all the consequences.

"Whatever happens, I cannot disappoint or ignore Vinny's ambitious plans of expanding the business. Surely I can't reveal my vexation with Lena" Visu's guiltiness is visible. "This is the job of thick-skinned fellows. I guess I have to become one." He started preparing his mind for any eventuality.

To get to files of Krish would not be that difficult for him, because of his intimacy with Krish and Lena; but he resented the idea that he has to stoop to such low level to perform an act of stealing. Several thoughts crossed his mind.

Vinny looked at Visu for some tangible answer. Visu kept silent and appeared seriously thinking. Visu contemplated many ideas. He recollected her passion for good drink before beginning her rabid lusty sexual overtures. "Getting her drunk sounded easy, plausible, and practical.

"I can get her drunk and engage in good sex. In any case, Lena's habit is to beg for sex before and kick him after sex," a wicked grin surfaced on him.

"After she gets what she wants Lena would not care what happens to the world." "She would not even care to see if I am with her in the bed or left the room after the act is over," "Therefore I can do what I want, her objecting my curiosity is not an issue."

Vinny did not understand Visu's silence, inattentiveness, and his reticence.

"If you find it difficult do not mind my suggestion. I am not insistent" Vinny shook hands and left. As soon as Vinny left, Visu's thoughts stormed him; he felt lonely, fear gripped him.

"How do I deal with Lena? He repeatedly questioned himself. The very name and her sex overtures frightened him. He became restless, started walking up and down his living room. "Am I her male prostitute? He despised the very idea. "No. she herself is a bitch; she seduced me, she is the one pushing me into this illicit relationship" Visu searched his conscience which is questioning his moral credentials.

However, the oppressive weight of his guilt continued to bear him down.

After Vinny left, his appealing words echoed, sentiment of reverence overwhelmed Visu. "I must do this for Vinny's sake, not for my advantage," Visu tried pacifying his uncertain mind. Sex-surge is equally pulling him "It is more than ten days" he counted his days of abstinence. "If by any chance, I am caught by Krish I may well be bold and face the consequence" he appeared prepared for any eventuality. Visu's irresistible temptation and sex bravery overwhelmed moral or ethical values. It is well nigh impossible to set aside the lusty lovemaking with Lena his sex diva.

He could barely resist calling Lena, mustered courage, picked up the phone and found three missed calls from Lena. Voice mail from her sounded desperate "Please answer me Visu."

"Hardly few days back I was with you" he teased her "Not enough? he laughed loudly.

"Not really" she replied. He noted the gumption in her voice. "You disappointed me," She sounded accusing.

"Thank God I escaped" Visu laughed. "Krish would have killed me on the spot" he added a note of panic in his voice.

"He is not that manly," she paused and added, "He is good at rousing my passion - that is all." "He is ineffective in making love. I told you that before" she sounded edgy.

"Yes Visu, I need you. I don't care Krish."

"Don't you think he will be jealous," he reminded her of his fear of eventual danger.

"Don't mind him. In the first night itself, he failed. He knows he is ineffective as a husband." "He surely would ignore even if he sees us in the act. I guess he is aware that I am meeting you. He accepted his ineffectiveness," Lena reminded him of an earlier discussion.

"So you could come - as Krish is surely going away to Bombay tomorrow to meet Mr Mistry and his son. He won't be back until a few days" Lena coolly invited him. Those few words invigorated his desire to meet her instantly. Besieged by sex drive Visu experienced lightening like excitement. He paused for a while, gathered himself, playful smile adorned him. He quipped, "I get the bottle and you get the condom" he chuckled at his crudity.

"Krish located Sastry's son Kaavoori, in Boston - as promised by him to his father in Delhi; and casually introduced Lena to him. Kaavoori stunned by her beauty, exclaimed spontaneously "You are a beauty queen." "Thank you" Lena modestly acknowledged with a smile in response. Kaavoori could not stop admiring her beauty. He looked at Krish, complimented "You are made for each other. I hope you do not mind my comment" he cheekily smiled at Krish.

He looked at Lena and said, "Fortunately, this is America, your husband should not mind if friends like me admire your beauty. In India, that comment may be indecent and immodest if a stranger makes it. No matter what, I must once again say you are beautiful" Kaavoori spent a few more minutes with them. "I hope you two settle down well in Boston" he shook hands with Krish.

Before leaving Krish and Lena, Kaavoori met Visu who just came to greet Krish; Kaavoori looked at him rather closely and pointed a finger said, "I saw you many times in the Shopping Malls but first time to meet you." Visu acknowledged that he too was seeing him, shook Kaavoori's hands vigorously.

"I will be back soon, wait for me Visu" Krish accompanied Kaavoori up to the car to send him off.

Lena had a chance to signal Visu to leave at once. "You told me he is leaving tonight," Visu whispered. She waved her hands and asked him to quit. Visu waited for Krish. Krish returned in a few minutes after sending away Kaavoori. "I am glad I could catch you in time" Visu greeted him. "I heard you are leaving to Bombay tomorrow."

Visu did not wait for his reply. "I just came to convey my good wishes. Bon voyage and best of luck Krish" Visu shook his hands. "Visiting parents, I guess" Visu expected Krish to give him some lead. Krish kept him guessing; after a while, he replied abruptly "Company affairs." That answer did not allow Visu to pursue any more manipulation for specific information about the purpose of his visit to India. Krish appeared busy and gave an impression of his disinterest to continue his conversation. Sensing an ambience of indifference Visu stood up to leave. "It is getting late – I have to go, but tell me if I could be of any help," Visu offered.

"I guess Lena can manage" Krish turned his head towards Lena who showed little interest.

"Feel free, call me any time," he garrulously signed off before leaving them.

Visu went straight to Vinny's house after leaving Krish.

"I checked out the current situation; Krishnamachary is surely going to India - Vinay is right. He must be going there to convince Mistry's son and finalize the deal as Vinay reported. "What do you think we should be doing now? Visu looked at an astute and serious looking self-confident Vinny not for an answer but for guidance.

Vinny replied, "If at all we could manage to get an estimate of the size of the deal," looked at Visu vaguely. "If we get to know that number we could work our way with the agents of Kenn and Dunn. Unfortunately we have no idea of the quantum of the deal."

Visu listened to every word of Vinny; he cast away all the niceties, decided to go ahead with his plans. After reaching home, he thought of calling her but decided to wait. Although dissatisfied with Lena's obvious indifference he was confident that she would call him. His assessment proved right.

Not surprisingly, Lena rang up the following morning, "Krish left; how soon can you come? She sounded desperate. "I could come right away but for surety's sake should we not wait? Visu urged her to be cautious.

"Yesterday you showed no interest," Visu peeved by her indifference teased her. "You know I was pretending" Lena cheekily admitted.

"I must tell you this - Krish attempted to make love but he failed miserably. We both are frustrated." "Moreover, he did the worst thing; intensely stimulated me but could not perform" she made no secret of her bitterness. "Come tonight with that Rothschild's old wine and be a good boy" her audacious and cheeky but sexy tone got him intensely excited.

"You are good without Viagra," her compliment sounded like a forewarning. For a minute Visu set aside his moral confusion, developed heartless self interest. He remembered his sole objective. "I must obey Vinny. I must collect those papers concerning the Mistry deal," he resolved.

The weight of his soul-less, 'do or die' situation pressed him to think of the stealthiest act, "I will get her drunk and search the room for any of the papers Vinny needed." He shuddered to think that nothing important would be left in the room. "I must try any how" he garbled.

"Heady cocktail of Brown sugar and wine does the trick" he remembered the talk of one jail-mate he met during his illegal immigrant jail mate. He remembered the old acquaintance's reason for his jail term.

"I and my partner were main-line addicts of Heroin. I made a mistake; gave her an overdose; and I was sentenced for murder." The repentant addict confessed to him. The very thought gave Visu a chill through his spine.

He hated himself for such mean, stealthy thinking. However, his determination to help his mentor coupled with his sex-surge drove him to Lena that night. "All I need is a pinch of brown sugar. A heady mix of sex and wine are enough for Lena" he mulled.

He recounted his student days experience with heroin. "It is a nice feeling; I was sleepy but high for 24 hours." "The Beatles: John Lennon, George Harrison, Paul Mcartney were my idols in those days. They inspired most of our choices of fashion, food and fancies; Beatles were using some addictive drugs" Visu admitted that he was carried away by his 'idols'. "Yes I tried Heroin, it wasn't dangerous" he tried to subdue his conscience.

"It is immoral, reprehensible and dirty act, Mr Viswanathan (Visu)" his inner voice shouted at him.

"I am not doing it for personal reasons – I am doing this to please my mentor. I have to clear my indebtedness to him, should I not," he answered as though he is answering someone questioning him. "I have no other option but going ahead with my plan."

"Besides, I love her, I must please Lena" thus, resolute Visu defied his moral conscience got ready with his bottle and the pep medicine he bought from a drug peddler.

"Fill the glasses before I come back." "Let me taste the special wine you brought," she commanded loudly while hurrying to the toilet.

"The very sight of your beautiful body makes me forget everything" Visu praised her; prepared the glasses, added the 'sugar' he bought in her glass; filled the glasses to the brim before Lena returned from the restroom wiping her bottom.

Lena returned in few minutes and fell into his stretched arms and sat on his lap. He placed wineglass to her mouth. She placed his wineglass to his mouth. Lena giggled proposing toast, "To my husband's health." Lena noticed Visu's sarcastic smile.

"You don't need to sympathize with him. After knowing that he has EDF problem and his impotency Krish cheated you." He fuelled her fury against her husband. She drank all the wine in one gulp.

"What is happening my friend – you are not active" she commented and noticed his distraction.

"You are red hot" he exclaimed. "Waiting for you," she whispered reflecting her great expectation.

Visu understood the reason, "Stimulation followed by depression." "The trick is working. She will sleep soon" he estimated the onset of peak effect within half an hour. He noticed her erotic movements slowed down. By the time he got up, she was snoring.

After he released himself he got up, adjusted his dress and hurriedly but quietly opened and searched all the cupboards and wardrobes for papers; left the room calmly after kissing her sleeping body.

As usual, he walked away from the room placing "Do not disturb" tab on the handle. He decided to hand them over to Vinny at once.

Although tired, he drove to Vinny's house and handed the copies of the papers.

"I got the papers just now, you told me it is urgent; so I brought it to you straight away - so late in the night. Forgive my intrusion" Visu sounded apologetic.

"You are amazing Visu" Vinny patted his back. "Our company owes its success to you" he sincerely praised him.

"Now that we know the offer of Mistry's of India, we will settle the deal with much better offer. I am going to go to NY right away; mobilize our contacts and seal the deal within this week. I know how to do it."

"We are talking big Visu" Vinny appeared highly elated.

"If we strike the deal we might enter billionaires club," he remarked with great jubilation. They shared a hearty laugh and had champagne to drink until midnight.

"I will clinch the deal before your friend returns from Bombay" assured Vinny.

"Vinny is a man of action" "Vinny is a man from rags to riches." In fact, he never stopped admiring him. "After all, share markets are the biggest gambling places. He must be a master gambler." "I do not know how he gets to know all the top movers" Visu wondered many times. He even talked to Warren Buffet in his presence. "Whatever it took he did everything legally possible to amass wealth. He gave me all the wealth I possess today, I owe him a lot" he saluted him in his mind; left Vinny's home in a jubilant mood. "Thank you Lena" he vocalized in ecstasy.

"It all happened because of Lena, the other name of pleasure," he felt immensely grateful to her. "She is a bag full of sex goodies."

"I wish I could marry her if Krish divorces her" the thought made him less guilty of his intimacy. He did not rate her high but thought of Lena as a possible wife. He assured himself, "I gave her what she wanted. I got what I wanted." "I will certainly consider marriage if we continue our relationship."

"She thoroughly enjoyed my sexability." He felt proud of himself.

Receptionist in Krish's office lazily picked up the phone that kept ringing; abruptly replied "Krishnamacharyulu saab is engaged in a serious meeting with his clients. He asked us not to disturb him during the meeting. Please call later."

"No" shouted the hotel manager. "It is very urgent. His wife was found dead in our hotel in Boston" yelled at the receptionist.

"Oh my God; are you sure? Saab just got married only a few months back" she rushed to Greg Mathiesen, the Managing Director and informed him of the bad news.

"Are you sure? He double-checked the information; rang up the hotel in Boston to confirm and pressed the red telephone. Krish got alarmed "You must come to me immediately" Greg requested him in soft voice. Nevertheless, Krish sounded irritated at the interruption. Krish excused himself for the interruption, asked his client Mistry and his son to wait. "I will be back soon" he left the room accompanied by his secretary.

Greg received him at the entry of his office. He appeared very serious. "Sit down Krish; I want you to go back to Boston immediately, your wife is seriously ill in Boston. I made all the arrangements for to-night's flight to New York. In NY's JFK airport a chartered flight will be waiting to take you to Boston."

Krish turned pale as paper "She is very healthy when I left," he mumbled.

Many stray thoughts crossed his mind. The first one was "Did she try to commit suicide? He got a doubt. "Impossible", "She is very tough; she would not do such things" he pondered over all the possibilities.

"She is deeply disappointed with my manliness" he once confided in Kaavoori.

Greg sat next to him in the sofa placed his arm around Krish's shoulder and said, "I instructed our office fellows in NY to assist you all the way." Krish grasped the seriousness of the situation.

"Is she that serious" he looked at Greg gravely. Greg bent his head, tried to hide the real information, muttered in low voice "Be prepared for anything" he walked a few steps away from Krish hiding his face. His answer in Germanized English left Krish in no doubt. By then Greg knew that the hotel staff are suspecting murder.

"I do not know if her father was informed" Krish pulled out his mobile, rang up Ramlu. Since there was no response from his father-in-law, Krish rang up his father in Delhi. By then they were away for a holiday in Hong Kong. Since he was not in touch with them regularly, he had no idea of their program; they do not know I am in India" Krish appeared lonely and helpless.

Greg suggested if he should contact any of his friends in Boston. He tried contacting Visu, who did not respond either. "There is no point in talking to the hotel manager, they moved her to the hospital," Greg misled Krish.

By then he alerted the hotel staff not to reveal but wait for his arrival. "Let us release the news slowly to avoid the rude shock until he arrives." Greg accompanied Krish to the airport followed him upto check-in and urged the flight staff to take care of him during the flight.

"I would have come with you to Boston, but for the busy schedule..." Krish stopped him and said, "Don't worry Greg, I can manage."

⚜

Within hours after Lena's death Boston Police have arrested Visu as they suspected him as the main accused. CCTV of the hotel revealed that he was the last one that left the room. CCTV clearly showed Visu attaching the 'Do not disturb' tab on the door handle.

"We have your fingerprints all over the cupboard," the officer warned Visu. Visu readily admitted he had spent some intimate time with her. He described his plan in detail; how he planned to induce sleep with 'Brown Sugar' mixed with wine. He revealed the fact that he bought Brown Sugar from a person called 'Desmond the Devil'.

"You have poisoned her," officer shouted at Visu."That was not my intention" he said it in a resolute manner.

"What then? The questioning was hostile. "I went to her room to collect some important documents pertaining to my company's interest." He gave all the details. "Did anyone prompt you to do this" officers questioned him.

"No it is purely my planning, no one else is involved." He excluded Vinny and Krish.

"You had sex with her before or after she drank the wine."

"I gave her the wine mixture to induce sleep, not to kill her. We are in intimate love with each other; she desired me all the time. We were in intense love every time we met."

"Does her husband know about the affair?

"Lena told me that she informed her husband that she will seek her own avenues because of her husband's impotence." "I guess her husband knows about our affair." He appeared remorseless and not careful.

"I loved her more than my own self. I never knew the power of destiny; it is that cruel decision of my destiny: I should end her life; I killed her with my own hands, what more is there for me to lose." He cried bitterly mumbling some words.

"I promised her that I will marry her if she could get divorce from Krish" he wailed inconsolably, with frequent gasps. He covered his face with both hands and uttered some words in his own mother tongue.

"Please send me to gallows, let me accompany her in her death. I do not want to be separated from her." He sobbed loudly.

Courts heard prosecution witnesses the hotel staff, acquaintances of the victim Lena and her husband Krish. All of them pointed fingers at Visu.

Epilogue

It took nearly a year for the judge and jury to conclude that since Visu volunteered his confession of the crime he be punished for manslaughter and drug misuse. They agreed with the Defense Attorney that there was no intent for murder; imposed 10-year imprisonment in Boston prison.

Thus, discredited and devastated Visu left US as his jail term got commuted after 5 years of good behavior. He renounced active life in US and returned to India, reportedly died as destitute on the banks of Ganga in Varanasi.

Rani, the mother of Lena directed her anger at Krish; accused him of conspiracy. "You and Murli conspired and killed my daughter." She added a dramatic legal twist. Krish had to face criminal charges and prolonged litigation. Murli also faced her ire but Ramlu protected him.

However, Ramlu never pardoned himself for believing in Krish. "He cheated my daughter," he kept on complaining until his death, a few months after Lena's death.

Krish lost his job because of depression and self-dejection. Vinay (son of Appaji) the bank officer and Vinny the Sri Lankan stockbroker accused of abetting business malpractice escaped punishment for lack of evidence but lost their credibility.

Our 'walkers group' friends remotely connected with the main characters got the facts from Murli. Appaji, the father of Vinay was aghast to hear his son's misdeeds. Sarma felt sorry for Ramlu, "He does not deserve this; he is a gentle soul."

Murli concluded his narration with a grin on his face, "He faced the worst enemy in that spiteful Rani; but somehow got out of muddle, but was seriously mauled by the events. Murli tok deep breath, appeared relieved and said, After the Court proceedings and exoneration, I wanted to escape the unwanted attention from family and friends in Hyderabad my friends.

I concede it is wrong to say that the Sun is reluctant to peep through the clouds. In reality it is 'clouds' playing the hide and seeks games with the Sun. I guess Life is like that.

Nevertheless, the residents and beach walkers of Vizag-on-Sea warmly welcomed the enlivening early morning *sandhya*.